Apple Crumble Assault

The Drunken Pie Café Cozy Mysteries, Book Four

Diana DuMont

Copyright © 2019 Diana DuMont

All rights reserved.

CHAPTER ONE

"Look who has a bright blue ribbon around his neck," exclaimed Grams as she approached my pie booth at the Sunshine Springs Fall Festival. "Although, really, don't you think they should make first place ribbons hot pink or bright orange instead of this boring dark blue?"

I looked up to see my grandmother, whom I affectionately called Grams, approaching with my Dalmatian, Sprinkles. Sprinkles did indeed have a bright blue first-place ribbon pinned to his neon orange collar. The collar had been a gift from Grams, and matched her neon orange hair. She was the most eccentric person I knew, especially for someone her age, and it didn't surprise me one bit that she would have preferred a neon orange or hot pink ribbon.

"He really won?" I asked as I started cutting a piece of apple bourbon crumble for Grams. I didn't even bother asking if she wanted a slice. I knew she was always up for a slice of my pie, and I wanted to see what she thought of today's batch of pies that I'd made especially for the Fall Festival. I started to give her the pie, but nearly dropped it when a giant, dark brown shape that looked suspiciously like a bear came into my peripheral vision. Grams must have noticed how much the bear startled me, because she threw back her head and laughed.

"It's only a costume, dear. You'll probably be seeing quite a few costumes over the next half hour or so. The annual costume contest is starting soon."

I relaxed as I handed her the pie. "Of course. I forgot that was today."

Today was second day of the annual Sunshine Springs Fall Festival, and the entire two-day festival was packed with events. There had already been a hotdog eating contest, a fashion show, and a craft show. Now, the costume contest was coming up, and later tonight there would be a talent show. The pet show that Sprinkles had just won was a new event this year. I'd gone back and forth on whether to enter Sprinkles, but when Grams had begged me to be the one to enter and show him, I couldn't turn her down. She loved my dog almost as much as if he were a human grandchild, and she often helped me out by watching him when I was busy at my pie shop, the Drunken Pie Café. I figured if she wanted to be the one to show him, then letting her do so was a small price to pay for all the ways she always helped me out.

To be honest, I hadn't expected Sprinkles to win. True, he was a Dalmatian, so he was a naturally attractive dog with his flashy, spotted coat. But he wasn't always that well-behaved, and he didn't know many tricks other than eating pie. I'd been sure that some other, better-trained dog would have beaten him out for the prize. Apparently, I'd been wrong about that, and I should have known. Between Sprinkles' gorgeous coat and Grams' eccentric neon hair and neon-colored outfit, they were a hard duo to ignore.

I chuckled as I saw a woman in a peacock costume walk by, her elaborate getup of royal blue and emerald green feathers bouncing behind her as she pranced along.

"People are really going all out for this costume contest, aren't they?" I said to Grams as she took a bite of her pie.

Grams paused for a moment to savor the boozy apple crumble before looking back at me and nodding. "Oh, most definitely. It's always one of the most popular events at the fair."

I nodded slowly, watching as a human gumball machine walked by. I didn't have much experience with the Sunshine Springs Fall Festival, since this was my first year in Sunshine Springs. I'd lived in San Francisco before, but had only rarely come up to visit Grams. She liked to occasionally spend time in the city, so she'd preferred to visit me in San Francisco. But after a nasty divorce, I left behind my career as a lawyer in the city to open my own boozy pie café.

There had been some hiccups over the last few months, but overall the café was doing quite well. I often sold out of my boozy pies by the end of the day, and I was slowly gearing up for what promised to be a busy and profitable holiday season. Even though it was only October, and Christmas was still a little over two months away, I had already received several special orders for Christmas pies. And, of course, my booth here at the Fall Festival was doing quite well.

As if reading my mind, Grams glanced over the remaining pies, then grinned. "Looks like everyone has an appetite for pie today."

I grinned back and nodded. "It's been nonstop sales all day. This is the first small lull that I've had. I'm happy for the business, but I'm not going to lie: I'm exhausted. Running this booth by myself is hard work."

Grams nodded sympathetically. She knew that the one big struggle my pie shop had was that I hadn't been able to find a reliable employee to help me. For a while, my best friend Molly had stepped up to help, but she had her own job as head librarian at the Sunshine Springs Library, and she was currently far too busy there to have time to help me out. I had briefly had an employee named Ruby who had seemed at first to be a wonderful, dependable addition to the pie shop. But I didn't even want to think about how horribly that had all ended.

Grams didn't miss the scowl that had appeared on my face. She frowned at me, and glanced over the pies that remained at my booth. "Why don't you take a break, dear? You could close up for an hour, get yourself some lunch, and get off your feet for a bit. Everyone will understand, and you've sold enough pies that taking an hour off is not going to break the bank."

But I shook my head at Grams. "Maybe in a little while. Right now, the after-lunch rush is coming up. Everyone's going to want dessert, and then there'll be another afternoon rush of people who want a mid-afternoon pick-me-up. I don't want to miss those chances to sell pie."

Grams sighed and shook her head, causing her neon orange hair to bounce slightly as she did. "You've always been a bit too hard of a worker for your own good. You should relax and enjoy life a little now and then. That's what I'm about to do. I'm going to go parade Sprinkles around the festival so everyone can see his first place ribbon, even though it *is* a boring blue color. I want everyone to know how proud I am of my grand-doggie. He's going to go down in history as the first ever winner of the Sunshine Springs Fall Festival pet show."

Grams puffed her chest out in pride, and I couldn't help but laugh.

"You should definitely go parade him around. You've earned the chance to be a little proud. But before you go, how did you like that pie?"

Grams gave me a big thumbs up. "Ten out of ten. That apple crumble is the bees' knees."

I groaned. "Grams, nobody says 'the bees' knees' anymore."

She shook her finger at me. "Not true. I still say it, and I'm not nobody. And now, if you'll excuse me, I've got a handsome, prize-winning Dalmatian to show off. Toodles."

Grams gave me a small wave and started to walk off. I waved back with a smile, shaking my head at her self-assured, fun-loving manner. I'd really won the grandmother lottery with her. As she walked off, someone in a Cruella de Vil costume walked by, and Sprinkles growled. I laughed, and then turned my attention back to my pie booth.

A few more customers came and went, and then, a familiar face suddenly popped into view.

"Theo!" I exclaimed. "I thought you'd be busy at the Sunshine Springs Winery booth."

Theo Russo, the handsome, wealthy owner of the Sunshine Springs Winery, grinned at me. "I took a break, and you should, too."

I groaned. "Now you sound like Grams. She was just over here, yelling at me that I work too hard. But, unlike you, I don't have a bunch of employees to cover for me while I'm gone."

"That doesn't mean you don't deserve a break."

I groaned again. "And now you *really* sound like Grams."

Theo's grin only widened. "Good. I like your grandmother. She's smart. Not only does she tell you to take breaks, she's also smart enough to realize that you should date me. I would say she's practically a genius."

"You're insufferable," I told him. It was true what he'd said about Grams. She was always trying to get me to date Theo. She told me I was never going to find a man as handsome and wealthy as him again, so I should snatch him up right away. She was probably right about that, but it didn't matter. I wasn't ready for a relationship right now. I looked up at Theo with an annoyed glare. "Did you just come here to irritate me? Because I'm too busy for these shenanigans."

Theo held up his right hand, which I now saw had a bright red candy-coated apple in it. "I actually came to bring you this. I was hoping you might walk with me for a bit and enjoy this apple. But it doesn't look like I'm going to have much luck getting you to leave this booth."

"No, sorry. I'm not leaving right now. But you're welcome to hang out for a few minutes while I eat my apple."

I made a grab for the apple, and Theo sighed as he willingly gave it up. "I should force you to walk with me before I let you have this, but I know how stubborn you are. You'll just tell me to keep my apple and shove it up where there's no sunshine."

I put one hand on my hip, and with the other hand I shook the apple in his direction. "Theo Russo! That's no way to talk to a lady."

Theo looked only mildly chastised. "I suppose not. But don't act like you wouldn't say something like that."

I merely laughed in his direction, and took a giant bite from the apple. Its sticky sweetness filled my mouth with sugar, and my heart with memories of fall. Candy-coated apples had always been my favorite as a child. Eating one now brought back happy memories of times with my parents—who had unfortunately passed away while I was in college. At least I still had Grams to make memories with. She might be up there in years, but she didn't show signs of slowing down anytime soon.

I closed my eyes for a moment to savor the apple and the memories, but a moment later I opened them again when I heard the familiar sound of my best friend's laughter. I looked up to see Molly approaching my pie booth. She was wearing a red cape, and Scott, who was her boyfriend and also one of my good friends, was dressed as a wolf. I laughed as I realized that their costumes were meant to be little red riding hood and the big bad wolf. They both giggled and occasionally stole quick kisses from each other as they made their way toward the pie booth.

"Here come the two lovebirds," grumbled Theo.

I ignored his sour attitude. I knew he was jealous that Scott had a girlfriend when he didn't. Even Molly had tried to convince me to date Theo so that I could go on double dates with Scott and her, but I wasn't interested.

"Clever costume," I said as they approached the booth.

"Thanks," Molly said. "Although I doubt we're going to win the costume contest. I can't believe how creative some of the costumes I've seen have been."

"You never know," I said encouragingly. "Do you two want some pie before you head off to the contest?"

"I'd love a slice of the apple bourbon crumble," Scott said, and Molly nodded in agreement. I cut slices of pie for them, and cut one for Theo as well without bothering to ask if he wanted one. I knew he would, even though he'd been in a grumbling mood. He would never say no to the chance to eat pie, or the chance to hang out with me for a few more minutes. As Scott, Molly, and Theo started in on their pie, I served another handful of customers. When there was another lull, I took another bite of my candy apple and then turned to Scott.

"So, any good gossip to share from the festival, or are you off duty today?"

We all laughed at this. Scott was the town's deliveryman, and odds were good that if you had a package coming in, he'd be the one bringing it to you. Because he spent his days buzzing around the town of Sunshine Springs, he always knew the latest gossip. But even though he wasn't working today, we all knew he'd be keeping his ears open for good gossip. He couldn't help it. He always wanted to know what the latest scoop was.

But it was Molly who answered for him. "We did see Tiffany and Jenny getting into a big catfight."

"Oh?" I said. "Let me guess: over Big Al Martel?"

"Bingo," Scott said around a mouthful of pie.

Big Al Martel had made a name for himself as a Hollywood star in numerous action films. He was currently one of the hottest names in Hollywood, except he didn't live in Hollywood. A few years ago, he'd made a big stink about how the whole town of Los Angeles was fake, and that there were better places to live in California.

He'd made a big show of moving to San Francisco, and had spent quite a bit of time there. I'd spotted him a few times around town when I lived in the city, and he was usually being followed by a gaggle of screaming girls. But I never understood the fascination with him.

Sure, he was rich, and I guess he was an okay actor. But he wasn't even that good-looking, and he came across as a bit of a jerk. I guess

I shouldn't judge him, since I didn't know him that well. But every time I saw him, he walked with a swagger that said he thought he was God's gift to the universe. Definitely not my type.

I hadn't seen him for a while, since I'd moved to Sunshine Springs. But a few weeks ago, he'd suddenly shown up in our sleepy little wine town. At first, everyone had thought he was just out for a weekend visit, but it soon became apparent that he was interested in more than just visiting Sunshine Springs. He wanted to open a restaurant in the town, and had been scouting out locations. Maybe he didn't think he had enough money from movies, or maybe he didn't think he was busy enough already as an actor. Whatever the reason, he wanted to add "businessman" to his résumé.

Over the last few weeks, he'd been in Sunshine Springs quite a bit, and had even been looking at some houses to buy. Apparently, he now thought that San Francisco, like Los Angeles, was too cliché of a place to live, and he was ready to move on.

Inevitably, he'd attracted quite a following of single, young women in Sunshine Springs. Tiffany Glover and Jenny Gullie were his current favorites, but the fact that he couldn't choose between them had become a problem. He'd be seen kissing one of them at dinner, and then later that same day someone would spot him smooching with the other one over dessert. Naturally, instead of being angry at Big Al over this, Tiffany and Jenny hated each other. They were both convinced that their man was being stolen from them, and Big Al, being the classy man that he was, seemed to enjoy being fought over. He took great pleasure in egging them on.

"What happened today?" Theo asked.

"Oh, it was a full-on catfight," Molly said. "They were pulling each other's hair, spitting at each other, and Tiffany even threw a glass of red wine at Jenny."

"Wow," I said. "Throwing red wine is the ultimate catfight move."

"Tell me about it," Molly said. "It was quite a sight. Eventually, someone pulled them apart. But for the most part, everyone stood and gawked. It was hard not to, honestly. They were really going at it."

I nodded. "I bet they were. I've seen them around town, glaring at each other, or, if the other one is not around, talking smack about each other. Sounds like their little feud is getting more and more out of control."

Molly swallowed another bite of pie. "Yep."

I frowned as I thought about this. "To be honest, I can't believe how much they fight over Big Al. Sure, he's wealthy and famous, but he doesn't even look that good. And he's such a jerk!"

"Yeah," Scott said. "If you ask me, all he's done is cause trouble in Sunshine Springs. Ever since he started spending more time in town, we've had to deal with a constant barrage of media reporters. Life has been quite disrupted."

I couldn't help feeling a little bit smug. "I tried to tell everyone that having a celebrity in town is not always as great as you think it's going to be, but no one listened to me, did they?"

"I listened," Theo said. "I never cared about him from the beginning."

I shrugged. That was true enough. Theo had always been pretty unimpressed by Big Al, and the more time Big Al spent in Sunshine Springs, the less impressed Theo seemed to be. In fact, the less impressed everyone seemed to be.

"Honestly?" Molly said. "I think everyone thought it was fun to have a celebrity around at the beginning, but at this point Jenny and Tiffany are the only ones who really want him to stay in town."

"*I* want him gone, that's for sure," a loud voice called from my right.

I looked over to see Bruce Burnham approaching. Bruce owned one of the more successful restaurants in Sunshine Springs—well, at least what *had* been one of the more successful restaurants in Sunshine Springs. Big Al had eaten there, claimed he got food poisoning from Bruce's food, and had taken his story to the media.

The media was happy to carry any story that had anything to do with Big Al, and a story about potential food poisoning had proven especially popular. Bruce had tried to fight back, saying that Big Al had provided no proof, and that no one else had claimed to be sick after eating at the restaurant that night. But it didn't matter what Bruce said. In the eyes of the world, Bruce was just some run-of-the-mill restaurant owner, and Big Al was Hollywood's golden boy. Why would anyone listen to Bruce over Big Al?

I felt badly for Bruce, but I didn't want to get into a discussion with him about how much he hated Big Al. I'd made the mistake of sympathizing with him when he came into the pie shop one day, and it had taken me a full thirty minutes to peel myself away from him. I couldn't afford to spend thirty minutes ranting about Big Al right now, no matter how much of a jerk he had been to Bruce.

So instead, I pasted a wide smile on my face and picked up my pie slicer.

"Pie?" I asked in a chipper voice.

Bruce frowned and looked over what I had on offer. "No strawberry moonshine pie today?"

I shook my head apologetically. "No, sorry. I sold out of that about half an hour ago."

Bruce frowned. "I was afraid that was going to happen. I couldn't get away from my restaurant's booth soon enough to get over here and grab some. I guess I'll take some of that rhubarb rum pie."

"You got it," I said, and handed a slice over to him. As he reached for his wallet, I shook my head. "Don't worry about it. It's on the house."

"Oh, come on. I insist," Bruce said.

But I shook my head again. "Really, I know how hard you've been working down at your restaurant booth. So take this as my gift to you from one vendor to another."

Bruce's face lit up with a smile, and that made me smile. No one could resist smiling when presented with free pie, and I was glad that I'd made his day a little bit better. I didn't know whether there was any truth to Big Al's claims of food poisoning at Bruce's restaurant, but from what I'd seen of Big Al, he didn't seem like the most trustworthy person. I knew Bruce took great pride in his restaurant. It was hard for me to imagine that he would serve food that wasn't perfect.

Apparently, I wasn't the only one who felt this way. As Bruce walked off, Theo remarked, "I bet Big Al made up that story about Bruce's restaurant to try to put him out of business."

"You really think he'd stoop that low?" I asked, even though I knew the answer to my own question. Big Al would stoop as low as he needed to in order to line his own pockets. He didn't care about Bruce, or Bruce's restaurant. Maybe that was the reason no one liked him in Sunshine Springs. Here in our small town, we helped each other out. Sure, each restaurant might technically be in competition with each other, but we understood that there was enough business to go around. And we all believed in the golden rule of doing unto others what you wanted them to do to you. That's how you got ahead in business around here—not by faking food poisoning scandals.

Scott opened his mouth as though he was about to contribute to the conversation, but he never got out whatever it was he was going to say. Before he could speak, he was suddenly interrupted by loud screeches. I'd never heard anyone sounding quite so loud, and I felt my body instantly tensing up. I glanced over at Theo, Scott, and Molly, and saw that they looked just as worried as I did.

"What in the world was that?" Molly asked. "It didn't even sound human."

The sound of more screeching reached my ears, and Molly was right. It didn't exactly sound human, except that if you listened closely one could tell that it was indeed human.

So why was someone making a noise like that? I felt my heart pounding in my chest, but I forced myself to turn and look in the direction of the screeching sound.

CHAPTER TWO

"You have got to be kidding me," Scott said.

If the expressions on the faces around me could be trusted, he'd spoken for all of us. Theo, Molly, and myself all had gone from looking worried to looking completely exasperated.

The inhuman screeching had apparently been caused by the appearance of Big Al Martel. A group of women ranging from teenagers to nearly my grandmother's age were following him as he sauntered across the festival grounds, an expression of smug satisfaction on his face.

"What is he even wearing?" Molly asked.

It was a good question. He looked like he was going for a cross between a tourist on vacation in Hawaii, a rapper from a big-city, and a model in an Armani cologne ad.

I shook my head. "He does have his own style, that's for sure." Then, I swallowed back my annoyance when I realized that he appeared to be walking straight toward my booth. "Is he heading this way?"

I felt my heart drop. Now I was really wishing I had heeded Grams' advice and closed the booth for a while. Then I might have missed him. Ordinarily, I had the policy of not turning away a paying customer, no matter what. But the obnoxious expression on Big Al's face tempted me to make an exception to that policy and refuse to serve him pie.

I was too polite to actually do that, of course. So, as he approached, I pasted a steely smile onto my face.

"Well," Scott said quickly. "Looks like it's time for us to go. As much as I'd love to stay and rub shoulders with a celebrity, the costume contest will be starting soon."

I glared at him, but I couldn't blame him. If I'd had a way to get out of talking to Big Al, I would have escaped, too.

"Good luck with the costume contest," I said with a sigh.

Molly reached across the counter to give my arm a quick squeeze. "Thanks, and good luck with Big Al. At least he's bound to bring some excitement into your day."

I watched Molly and Scott wandering off, both of them stealing occasional kisses from each other. Molly even stopped to pull out her cell phone and take a selfie of Scott and her, which wasn't surprising since she had an obsession with selfies. I was sure that her online photo albums would be full of new festival selfies later tonight.

I turned to look at Theo. "Are you abandoning me, too? I can't say I blame you if you do."

The screeching was getting louder by the moment. I could see now that Big Al was being trailed not only by a gaggle of screaming girls, but also by several reporters and photographers who were no doubt hoping to catch a unique shot of him that could be sold to one of the celebrity gossip magazines for a boatload of money.

"I'll stay," Theo said grudgingly. "But only because I like you so much." Then he winked at me. "I have to stick around so I can intervene if you start making googly eyes at Big Al. I'm definitely not letting him win your heart over."

I snorted. "Trust me. You don't have to worry about that. Obnoxious and rude is definitely not my type."

Big Al had nearly reached the pie booth by that point, so I shut my mouth and forced myself to keep smiling in his direction.

"Good afternoon, Mr. Martel," I said. I decided it was better to keep things as formal as possible, so I referred to him by his last name instead of as "Big Al." Apparently, this annoyed him, and he frowned at me.

"Well, good afternoon to you, you pretty young thing. Don't go breaking my heart by speaking so formally to me." He leaned forward to try to get his face close to mine, and I slowly leaned back. Beside Big Al, I could see that Theo was clenching his teeth together and had a stiff expression on his face. I wouldn't put it past Theo to launch a punch at Big Al, and I definitely didn't want that. Not only would it cause chaos at my pie booth, which would certainly result in lost sales, but I also had a feeling that Big Al would gleefully sue anyone who dared mess up his precious little face. I shot Theo a warning glare, and turned my attention back to Big Al.

"That's very kind of you, Mr. Martel," I said, emphasizing my words as I spoke his last name. "But I do like to be sure that I'm respecting the formality of the customer relationship. What can I get for you today?"

Big Al must not have been as dumb as I thought he was, because he looked from me to Theo, and understanding seemed to dawn on his face. He must have figured out somehow that Theo had a thing for me, and he must have thought that's why I wasn't interested in him.

All around the pie booth, Big Al's legions of female fans were still trying to catch his attention, and I wanted to tell him to choose one of them. Any of those women would gladly have called him by any name he wanted to be called.

But I forced myself to smile at him, and gestured toward the pie. I didn't want to make a scene with this many reporters, tourists, and fans present. I was bound to look petty if I started something with Big Al, and I didn't want my pie shop to be associated with petty.

"Can I interest you in a complementary slice of pie?" I asked in a sugary-sweet voice. I wasn't in the habit of always giving away so much free pie, but sales today had been good. I was hoping that getting something for free would appease Big Al into thinking that I actually cared about his celebrity status and was impressed by it.

Apparently, free pie did make him happy, because a grin spread across his face. "I'd love a slice of your pie, Isabelle," he said as he squinted at the name on one of my business cards that I'd placed on the table in front of me. I didn't bother to correct him and tell him that everyone in Sunshine Springs called me Izzy, even though my proper name was on my business cards. I didn't want to encourage him into thinking that we were on a nickname basis.

He got a greedy look in his eyes, and looked over the many pies I had on offer. "What do you recommend?"

I quickly contemplated the pies that remained. I had sold out of my lemon vodka pie and strawberry moonshine pie already, which surprised me since those were summer flavors. I'd thought they wouldn't sell as well at a fall festival, but I'd been wrong about that.

The apple bourbon crumble was still going strong, since I'd made plenty of those. I also still had some death by chocolate pie, which was made with red wine from Theo's winery. I had yet to meet anyone who'd tried that pie and didn't like it, so I decided it was a safe bet to recommend to Big Al.

"If you like chocolate, I highly recommend my death by chocolate pie. It's become a Sunshine Springs classic, because it's made with red wine from our very own Sunshine Springs Winery."

I shot Theo a smile, and he grinned back. He was probably remembering, like I was, how the death by chocolate pie had come to be. When I'd first moved to Sunshine Springs, Theo and I had both been caught up in a murder case. We'd both been suspects for a while, which at first had made us enemies, but had then turned us into friends. In the end, when we were both proven innocent and the real murderer was found, I'd created the death by chocolate pie using the wine from his winery as a way to commemorate our new friendship.

But Big Al wasn't interested in commemorating our friendship. He scowled when he saw the smile passing between Theo and me, and he pointed down at the death by chocolate pie.

"Sure, I'll try slice of that, even though I'm not a fan of Theo's wine. It's too bitter, if you ask me. But if anyone can make that wine into something good, I'm sure it's you, Isabelle. Word around town is that you know how to make a good pie."

"I can assure you that this pie is delicious," I said stiffly, "Just like the wine from Sunshine Springs Winery."

Big Al snorted. "We'll see about that."

As he took a bite, I heard the popping of paparazzi cameras, and I did my best not to groan out loud. I didn't want my pie shop to be tangled up in any kind of Big Al news, regardless of whether he liked or didn't like my pie. I just wanted him to leave me alone.

There were a few moments of silence as Big Al chewed his bite of pie. Even the women who had been following him and screeching quieted down, holding their breath as though waiting to hear Big Al's opinion of my pie was the most exciting thing they'd done in their lives thus far. Big Al enjoyed this attention, and he made a big show of chewing slowly and thoughtfully.

After an unreasonably long dramatic pause, he finally smiled and said, "Well, Isabelle, I think you've got yourself a winner there. You

Apple Crumble Assault

have indeed managed to do the impossible: you've made Theo's wine into something good."

Cheers went up from the fans surrounding Big Al. He ate up the attention as he ate up his pie. Predictably, all of Big Al's entourage suddenly had to have slices of the death by chocolate pie as well. For the next fifteen minutes, I sold slice after slice, until I was sold out of that flavor completely. When the last slice was sold, I breathed a sigh of relief, and looked over to find that Theo was still standing there, looking as ticked off as I'd ever seen him.

"That man is a disgrace to humanity!"

I reached over to put a sympathetic hand on his shoulder. "Don't let him get to you. Bruce is right, you know? He's just trying to bring down everyone in town besides him. He thinks that's the way to do business."

Theo looked over at Big Al and grunted in annoyance. The man was still working on his slice of pie, taking his time and freely blowing kisses to the women around him.

As Theo and I watched the ridiculous scene unfolding around Big Al, someone in a full monkey costume walked up to the pie booth. I had been planning to share more not-so-kind observations about Big Al with Theo, but I clamped my mouth shut as the monkey approached. It was impossible to tell who was underneath the costume, and you definitely didn't want to complain about Big Al when the wrong person might hear. It wouldn't help matters at all to have something about Theo hating Big Al end up in the celebrity gossip rags. I could just see the headlines now: "Local Winery Owner Feuds with Hollywood Celebrity."

The monkey walked up to my table and appeared to be looking over the pie options—although I couldn't say for sure what the monkey-person was looking at, because his or her eyes were completely hidden by the costume.

"Isn't the costume contest starting already?" I asked the monkey.

In response, all I got was an "Ooh-ooh-ahh-ahh."

I had to stop myself from rolling my eyes. "Right. Well, can I get you some pie?"

"Ooh-ooh-ahh-ahh," the monkey said again, and pointed to one of my apple bourbon crumbles.

"You want a slice of apple bourbon crumble?"

The monkey-person shook his or her head no, and exclaimed,

"Ooh-ooh-ahh-ahh!" Then the monkey made a big circular motion with his or her monkey hands. I frowned, trying to understand.

Theo laughed. "I think the monkey wants to buy the whole pie."

"Ooh-ooh-ahh-ahh," the monkey said excitedly, nodding his or her head up and down.

"Alright, the whole pie it is."

I carefully placed the pie in a pie box and wrapped it up with a custom-made Drunken Pie Café ribbon. I'd ordered the ribbons when I first opened my café, and hadn't had much occasion to use them since most people opted to buy slices of pie instead of whole pies. Hopefully, I'd get some use out of the ribbons during the holiday season when people ordered whole pies for Christmas.

I placed the box on the table in front of the monkey. "That'll be thirty dollars even."

I was done giving away free pie for the day, and I especially wasn't giving a whole pie away to a crazy monkey-person. But the monkey didn't seem bothered by the price of the pie.

"Ooh-ooh-ahh-ahh," the monkey said, and then handed me three crisp ten dollar bills. I had to admit that I was a bit disappointed that the monkey hadn't paid with a credit card. I was hoping to see the name on the credit card and figure out who was behind this costume.

No such luck.

The monkey did a little jig, said, "Ooh-ooh-ahh-ahh" again, then picked up the pie box and walked off. I saw him already untying the ribbon as he walked away, and I asked myself again why I even bothered to spend the money on those ribbons.

"People really get into the costume contest around here, don't they?" I remarked to Theo, echoing the sentiment I'd already spoken to Grams earlier that day.

"Yep. It's always a circus around here during the Fall Festival. Although, this year the circus is bigger than most years." Theo pointed in the direction the monkey was walking. The furry creature appeared to be headed straight toward Big Al, who was still surrounded by a large group of fawning women. I noticed that not far past Big Al, Scott and Molly were still visible.

I frowned. "Scott and Molly are sure walking slowly for a couple who were in such a rush to get to the costume contest."

Theo merely grunted, apparently still not willing to discuss the two lovebirds at length. I decided not to push the subject, and turned my attention instead back to the "circus" in front of me. Big Al had long since finished his own slice of pie, but he was currently accepting bites of pie from the women around him, who were happy to share with him. I rolled my eyes and was about to turn away from the spectacle when I noticed that the monkey was standing fairly close to Big Al and fumbling to open the pie box from the apple bourbon crumble. I watched with interest, wondering what the monkey was doing.

Theo had noticed it, too. "Why doesn't he take off his monkey gloves for a moment? It would make opening that pie box a lot easier."

"The monkey might be a she, not a he," I pointed out. "It's impossible to tell beneath that costume. But yes, I agree with you. That monkey seems awfully committed to staying in character. And anyway, it's kind of weird to buy a whole pie and open it like that in the middle of the festival grounds. Is the monkey intending to share it with the whole group there?"

I watched with mild fascination as the monkey finally got the pie box open and pulled the pie out, letting the box fall to the ground. No one around him—or her, if the monkey was indeed a her—seemed to be paying much attention to the monkey and the pie. I supposed that wasn't that surprising. Even in the group of Big Al's fans, there were a few costumed characters still hanging around, apparently more concerned with rubbing shoulders with a celebrity than with making their way to the costume contest.

The monkey carefully balanced the pie in one monkey hand, and I watched closely to see what he or she would do. Then, in the next moment, I gasped as I saw the monkey lift the pie and bring it forward, smashing it square in Big Al's face.

For a brief moment, everything was quiet.

Then, the laughter started. Even from a distance, I could see Big Al's face turning purple with rage where his skin was still visible between the globs of apple bourbon crumble that clung to his skin. But his rage didn't keep the crowd around him from doubling over with laughter, and I couldn't keep a giggle from bubbling up in my own throat. If you asked me, Big Al Martel was just getting what was coming. He couldn't constantly treat people the way he did and expect everyone to just take it. Now, I understood why the monkey hadn't wanted to reveal his or her identity. He or she didn't want to risk Big Al's wrath, so staying anonymous as a monkey was the perfect plan. Big Al would have no way of knowing who had actually pied him in the face.

Beside me, Theo let out a chuckle as well. But then, our laughter died in our throat, as did the laughter of everyone else surrounding Big Al. As I watched, hardly believing my eyes, the monkey reached into what must have been a pocket in the monkey suit, pulled out a large knife, and drove it straight into Big Al's chest.

Big Al yelped in pain, and a moment later fell to the ground in a lifeless heap. For a few seconds, everything was completely quiet as everyone else stared on in shock.

Then, the chaos started. The women surrounding Big Al started screaming and running away in terror. The paparazzi started snapping pictures of the scene, and some more folks who had initially not been interested in Big Al at all were suddenly running over to see what was going on. Several people started yelling that he'd been stabbed, which brought more folks over to look.

I looked over at Theo, who was gaping at the scene in shock. But after a few moments, he snapped out of that shock and jumped into action.

"Izzy, call an ambulance," he called over his shoulder, already starting to run toward Big Al. "I know CPR. Maybe I can still do something to help him."

I followed closely behind Theo, reaching for my cell phone to dial 911.

But when I got to the scene of the crime and saw how still Big Al's body was lying, I had a feeling that no ambulance was going to be able to save him.

CHAPTER THREE

When I reached Big Al's body, I took one look, then turned away in horror from the sight. He was definitely dead.

As I turned, I came face-to-face with Molly, who was looking just as pale as I must have.

"What happened here?" she asked. "One moment Scott and I were taking selfies. This person in a monkey costume smashed a pie in Big Al's face, which we happened to catch in the background of one of our selfies. Then, a few moments later, as we were looking at the pictures on my phone and laughing, we heard screaming. We looked up and everyone was running in different directions, and now Big Al looks quite dead."

Molly peeked past me for a moment, then quickly looked away. She must have decided, as I had, that it was better not to look.

"That monkey stabbed Big Al!" I said. Then I looked around frantically, suddenly realizing that the monkey didn't seem to be around anymore.

"Oh no! No one stopped him!" I scanned the crowd, trying to find the monkey. Tons of costumed characters had appeared on the scene. Close to me, I saw a jellyfish costume, a green army man costume, and a fairy costume. Beyond that, I saw a superman costume and a mermaid costume—among others. But there was no monkey to be seen.

I smacked my forehead. "We were all so shocked in the moment that I don't think anyone tried to grab the monkey. Now he's gotten away. Or maybe I should say *she*. I'm really not sure which it was, since you couldn't see anything in that costume, and the monkey refused to say anything except 'ooh-ooh-ahh-ahh' in a strange voice."

Now, the monkey's insistence on staying completely in costume made perfect sense. With so many people already dressed up at the festival, no one thought twice about someone walking around in a full monkey costume, and the monkey gloves would have kept any fingerprints from getting on the pie box or anything else the monkey might have touched in the course of committing this murder. Now, no one had any clue who he or she was. It was the perfect plan.

Just then, shouts sounded out as the paramedics arrived and pushed their way through the crowd. Some paramedics had been on the festival grounds in a medical emergency tent, and they had arrived before the ambulance. Theo stood to get out of their way, and came to stand by me, shaking his head sadly as he did.

"It's no use," he said softly as he watched the paramedics starting to check Big Al's vitals. "That monkey got him good. He's a goner."

I watched in disbelief, trying to process what had just happened. The crowd around us was only growing, as word must have been spreading across the festival grounds of what had happened. More and more costumed characters arrived as well, and I had a feeling that the costume contest was going to be delayed, if not canceled altogether. The paparazzi continued to take photos, and several local news reporters who had already been around the festival grounds abandoned whatever other projects they were doing to come see if they could get a head start on reporting what was sure to be the biggest news around here for quite some time.

I felt my stomach turn as I realized that it wasn't just the paparazzi and the media taking photos. Many people had pulled out their cell phones and were snapping shots of the lifeless heap that was all that remained of Big Al Martel.

I looked over at Theo and wrinkled my nose. "Don't people have any respect? Big Al wasn't my favorite person, but it seems crass to me to take pictures of a body like that—like he's some kind of festival exhibit."

"Agreed," Theo said. "People have no boundaries these days."

I shook my head, thinking that it was bad enough I'd seen all of this in person. I definitely didn't want a photographic reminder of the awful sight.

In fact, I had seen quite enough of this sight as it was. "I'm out of here," I said as I turned on my heel. I glanced at Molly. "Want to come with me? I think I might close down the pie shop and call it a day."

Molly nodded, and glanced at Scott. "Want to come with us?"

Scott nodded and turned to go with us. I glanced over at Theo to ask him if he wanted to come too, so that he wouldn't feel left out. But before I could say anything, he raised an eyebrow at me.

"You're not going to stay around and hope for clues?" he asked.

I sighed. If this had happened a few months ago, I would have been eager to put my amateur sleuthing skills to work. I would have done my best to figure out who had been behind the monkey costume, and behind Big Al's death. But a little over a month ago, I had promised Sheriff Mitchell McCoy, the Sheriff in Sunshine Springs, that I would give up playing detective. He'd been worried, as had Molly, that chasing after murderers was too dangerous, and that I was going to get hurt—or worse. After a few attempts on my life, I decided they were right, and I promised them both to lay off on the sleuthing.

And, to be honest, although I couldn't deny that I was a tiny bit curious who was behind the monkey costume, this was one case I definitely didn't want to get wrapped up in. I could already tell that this investigation would turn into a media circus. So, I shook my head and shrugged my shoulders.

"No, I'm not touching this case with a ten foot pole. Let's go. I'll pack up my pie booth, and if the city does leave the festival open despite what just happened here, maybe we can all actually enjoy a little time together."

Even as I said it, I knew it wasn't likely. My guess was that the police would shut down the festival now that there was a crazy, murderous monkey on the loose. Besides, it was probably a bit unrealistic to think that we could have a good time knowing that someone had been killed here just a short time ago.

But I figured I would just start with packing up my pie booth and see how things played out from there.

My thoughts were interrupted by the sound of shouting from a very familiar voice.

"Out of the way! Out of the way! Everyone move back! You're contaminating a crime scene!"

I felt a rush of relief when I heard Sheriff Mitchell McCoy's voice.

He was known to everyone in Sunshine Springs as Sheriff Mitch, or simply "Mitch," and he had become one of my best friends—despite the fact that we'd initially gotten off on the wrong foot. He'd accused me of murder when I first arrived in his town, but I'd been proven innocent in that case. Now, Mitch and I were close friends. So close, in fact, that he had tried to date me. That was sort of funny, since he and Theo were best friends. But their rivalry for me hadn't seemed to affect their friendship.

Not that it mattered if they were both fighting over me, because I wasn't dating either of them. Still, I was happy to have them as friends. And I was happy that Mitch had arrived. No doubt, his presence would bring some order to the current chaos.

I scanned the crowd for Mitch, and I couldn't help bursting out into laughter when I finally saw him. Perhaps that wasn't the most appropriate thing to do, considering the gravity of the current situation, but I couldn't stop myself. Mitch was standing at the perimeter of the crowd and beginning to push his way through, but he wasn't wearing his police uniform. As he came into view, I could see that he was dressed like a pro wrestler—complete with his face painted black and white and a shiny blue wrestling uniform that sort of reminded me of a fancy loincloth.

Molly frowned at me, confused about why I was laughing. She followed my gaze, and started laughing as well when she saw Mitch. Soon, Scott and Theo were laughing, too.

Several people in the crowd turned to look at us, confused as to why we were laughing. They glanced at Mitch, but then shrugged. It probably wasn't as funny to see a man in a wrestling costume if you didn't know that he was actually the chief of police. But to me, Molly, Scott, and Theo, it was hilarious. I heard a few other people in the crowd starting to chuckle, and I knew that some other Sunshine Springs residents had seen and recognized Mitch. Most of the people in the current crowd, however, were tourists and were not aware that they were witnessing the police chief in all his wrestler glory.

Theo was laughing the hardest of all. "Well, well, well. I didn't know you were the wrestling type," he said as Mitch approached us.

Mitch glared at him. "I lost a bet with the guys at the station, okay? They forced me to wear whatever costume they chose for the costume contest, and apparently this was the best they could come up with."

Scott was trying to stifle back his laughter. "I'd say they did quite well. You look quite, um, realistic."

Mitch scowled at Scott. "It's not funny, and this isn't the time for jokes. I have a crime scene to secure."

Mitch started yelling again for everyone to back up, but everyone ignored him. No one took seriously the crazy man in the wrestler costume, until Theo, looking admittedly handsome and authoritative in his jeans and sport coat, raised his voice.

"This man is the Sheriff! You all better listen to him if you know what's good for you. Now, back up!"

The crowd quieted slightly, and looked at Mitch with interest. One of the tourists yelled out, "He don't look like no Sheriff to me!"

Mitch pulled his badge from his wrestler loincloth. I don't know how he'd managed to fit anything in there, but he must have had a pocket somehow. He flashed his badge and yelled out, "I am the Sheriff of Sunshine Springs. And unless you want to be charged with inhibiting a murder investigation, you'll get out of my way right now."

That did the trick. The crowd slowly backed away, although the paparazzi kept taking pictures—as did the people on their cell phones. More and more Sunshine Springs locals were arriving on the scene, and they dutifully listened to Mitch and stayed back, since they already knew who he was. But I could see the horror in their eyes as they whispered to each other. None of this seemed real. How was it possible that Big Al had been alive less than thirty minutes ago, sauntering around eating pie, and now he was lying in a heap on the ground, never to rise again?

A few moments after Mitch had finally gotten the crowd pushed back, the other police officers started to arrive. They quickly began consulting with Mitch, and they all ignored the shouts from the media and paparazzi asking for a comment on the situation.

Slowly, as it became evident that no more information was forthcoming, the crowd began to dwindle. I realized then that I was still standing there even though I'd planned to leave. I turned to look at Molly, and saw that she and Scott were also still watching as Mitch and his officers began to set up a yellow crime scene tape.

Just then, Mitch looked up and caught my eye. He often looked irritated when he was working on a case. I think it was just the way he concentrated. But right now, he looked especially irritated. His scowl only deepened as he looked at me.

I gulped as he started walking toward me.

"What are you still doing here, Izzy?" he asked. "Please don't tell me you're trying to find clues. You know how I feel about your interfering in my cases. And trust me: I am not in the mood for this right now."

I quickly shook my head to reassure him. "No, don't worry. I'm not trying to get involved. In fact, I was just about to leave when you arrived. I swear that I'm not trying to interfere. I just couldn't help it that I saw everything happen as it unfolded. My pie booth is right over there." I pointed back toward my pie booth, and Mitch grunted.

"Well, if you are leaving, then please leave. There are way too many people around here, and my officers need to be able to concentrate to gather evidence and talk to people who might have seen who did this." Mitch cracked his knuckles as he often did when he was excited about something.

I thought about telling him that I *had* seen something, but then I thought better of it. I doubted I had seen anything more than anyone else who been standing close to Big Al. Besides, I could always stop by and talk to Mitch at the station tomorrow, even though I was sure by then he would be well aware that this had all been perpetrated by someone in a full monkey costume.

As I turned to leave, though, the sound of loud, angry yelling reached my ears. I turned to look in the direction of the yelling, as did Mitch. Before I could even see through the crowd to determine what the fuss was about, Mitch groaned.

"Great," he said as he started to walk away from me and toward the yelling, suddenly losing interest in making sure that I left the scene. The last thing I heard him say before he was out of earshot was, "Here comes trouble."

CHAPTER FOUR

"No! It's *your* fault! If he had been safe with me, this never would've happened!"

I once again forgot about leaving the crime scene as I saw Tiffany Glover and Jenny Gullie both fighting their way through the crowd. They were alternating between attempting to land punches on each other and pushing aside tourists and festival-goers. My eyes widened as they approached the yellow crime scene tape with no indication that they planned to slow down. They were a split second away from breaking right through the tape when Mitch appeared right behind them. I watched as he grabbed each of them by the back of the neck, and dragged them backward.

"This is a crime scene!" Mitch roared. Even though he was quite far away from me at this point, I could still hear him clearly. So could everyone else. He completely lost his temper in that moment.

"Everyone back away from the tape! Back, back, back!"

Most people did as he asked, although there was some grumbling. Tiffany and Jenny, however, didn't seem interested in obeying his orders.

"I have a right to see him," Tiffany yelled. "He was my boyfriend!"

"No he was *my* boyfriend!" Jenny yelled.

"It doesn't matter whose boyfriend he was," Mitch said. "No one's touching him right now."

But Tiffany and Jenny ignored Mitch and tried to lunge forward again. His hands, which were still grabbing their shirts by the back of the neck, kept them from moving forward. But instead of turning on Mitch in anger, they turned on each other.

"This is all your fault!" Tiffany yelled again.

In response, Jenny lunged at Tiffany, trying to shove her. She missed for the most part, but Tiffany was spoiling for a fight and tried to shove her back. I could tell that Mitch, despite his strength, was having a hard time holding them. He might as well have been trying to hold two angry cats. He seemed to realize this, and let go of them in that moment. They lunged at each other, and were soon rolling on the ground in a ball of screams, scratches, and insults.

Mitch looked at them and shook his head wearily. Tiffany and Jenny, in their anger at each other, were actually rolling away from the yellow crime scene tape. Mitch seemed happy enough with that. He gestured toward one of his officers to keep an eye on them, and then moved back toward the actual scene of the crime. The crowd that remained at the crime scene was more interested now in watching the fight unfolding between Tiffany and Jenny than in staring at Big Al's body, which was not providing much entertainment anymore.

Big Al was now being photographed by someone who looked like an official crime scene investigator. The paparazzi, who had by now realized there were not going to be any new shots of Big Al to take, had moved on to taking shots of Tiffany and Jenny as they rolled around in the dirt. I winced as I glanced over and saw Tiffany quite literally pull a chunk of Jenny's hair out.

"They're just embarrassing themselves," I murmured.

"Yep, but it's not the first time today," Molly said.

I shook my head in disgust and started to turn to leave. "Okay, now I *really* want to get out of here."

But the circus wasn't over yet. As I turned, I heard the sound of a man sobbing and distraught. I looked up to see George Drake approaching.

George had lived in Sunshine Springs for about a decade. He'd made good money in real estate, not only in Sunshine Springs but also in the surrounding wine towns. He'd also invested in several restaurants and wineries across the region—investments that had given him enough money to never have to work another day in his life.

George and Big Al had been friends for decades, and from what

I'd heard, George was the reason that Big Al had visited Sunshine Springs in the first place. George had invited his friend to check out the town because he thought it was a good place for Big Al to start up on his investments into the restaurant industry.

Those investments would never be made now, but George clearly wasn't thinking about investments at the moment. I watched as he pushed his way through the crowd with a grief-stricken look on his face.

"It can't be true! Please, someone tell me that it's not true! He can't be gone!"

I winced as I saw him reach the front of the crowd. I knew the exact moment that he saw Big Al. Any remaining hope in his eyes disappeared, and storm clouds filled his expression.

"No!" he cried out. Then he lunged himself forward toward Big Al, ignoring the fact that the yellow crime scene tape was there. Luckily, one of the police officers caught him and held him back before he managed to break through.

"Let me go to him! You can't leave him alone like that on the cold, hard ground! I was the only true friend he had in this world. Let me see him!"

The police officer tried to speak to George in a soothing tone, but it clearly didn't do anything to change the fact that George was beside himself. He sobbed and continued to try to break free of the officer so that he could reach Big Al. I looked back and forth between George and between Tiffany and Jenny, who were still rolling around on the ground in a petty wrestling match. The media was eating up the moment. I heard the constant whirr of camera shutters in-between George's sobs and Tiffany's and Jenny's screams.

Then I saw Mitch walking over to try to reason with George. I wasn't sure what he said, but it seemed to have some effect. George at least stopped the loud sobbing and instead merely sniffled. George nodded a few times, and then Mitch pointed to one of the police officers.

But as soon as Mitch pointed to the officer, George seemed to lose whatever calmness he had found. He started gesturing wildly with his hands and yelling at Mitch and the officer. When the officer reached out to try to put a calming hand on George's shoulder, George swatted at him and then tried to push him away. Mitch held George back and started speaking to him again. Slowly, George calmed down and nodded, looking defeated at whatever it was Mitch was saying.

Realizing once again that I should have left a long time ago, I turned to Molly to ask her if she wanted to come. But when I turned to my right, I saw Sprinkles and Grams approaching. Grams had a worried look on her face, and Sprinkles was making a beeline for me, no doubt worried that I was in some sort of danger. He had been extra-protective of me ever since the criminal in the last murder case I'd worked on had made a few attempts on my life.

Grams reached out to touch my arm. "Izzy? What's going on? Is it true what I heard? Is Big Al really dead?"

I nodded at Grams. "Yep, it's true. Murdered by a monkey." Then I explained to her everything that had happened thus far.

"Goodness," Grams said, a nervous hand fluttering to the neckline of her bright green dress. I know Big Al wasn't everyone's favorite, but who would do such a thing?"

"I was wondering the same thing," I said. "Although, to be honest, right now I just want to pack up my pie booth and go home. I'm sure Mitch will get this all sorted out."

Grams opened her eyes wider in surprise. "You're not going to try to help him this time?"

I shook my head. "No. I really think it's better if I give up sleuthing. That last case left me a little gun-shy about being an amateur detective. Besides, I think Mitch would appreciate it if I lie low."

Grams shrugged. "He looks like he's definitely thinking *something* related to you, at any rate."

"What do you mean?" I asked, furrowing my brow.

"Look." Grams pointed toward where George was standing, and I saw that Mitch was making a beeline for where I stood.

I frowned, and even looked behind me to see if there was someone else there he might be interested in, like one of his officers, or one of the guys on the crime scene investigation team that was helping gather evidence. But there was no one behind me other than a rapidly thinning crowd of festival-goers.

Confused, I turned back toward Mitch, sure that I must be mistaken, and that he must be heading somewhere other than straight toward me. But now that he was even closer, there was no mistaking it. He was coming for me, and his gaze was fixed firmly on my face.

"Izzy," he said as he approached. "What are you doing right now?"

"Uh, nothing, really," I said a bit uncertainly. "I was about to go pack up my pie booth and probably head away from the festival grounds."

I felt a bit guilty, thinking that Mitch probably wasn't happy that I was still there, and probably thought that I was trying to interfere in the investigation despite my promises that I wouldn't.

"Can you take George home for me?" Mitch asked.

This question was so unexpected that my jaw literally dropped. "Uh…sure, I guess," I stammered out.

"I know it's a bit of a weird request," Mitch said, cracking his knuckles in frustration. "But George is beside himself and I need to get him away from the crime scene. He's agreed to go home if I promise to keep him updated on any leads we might have on Big Al's murderer. But when I tried to get one of my officers to take him, he freaked out and said he's not riding in a cop car where he's going to be interrogated about this. I promised him no one was going to ask him any questions and that he could always just come make a statement at the station tomorrow, but he's beside himself and hysterical. I asked him if it was alright if I had a civilian take him home and he seemed okay with that. He said if you can drive him home that he'll go with you."

"But I don't even know him," I said with a frown. "Why would he choose me?"

Mitch shifted uncomfortably from one foot to another. "I may have volunteered you," he admitted.

My eyes widened. "You volunteered me? But why? Normally you want me to stay as far away from your cases as possible."

"I know," Mitch said sheepishly. "But honestly, you were the first person that popped into my head. I don't know why. I'm under a lot of stress. Besides, I trust you. You might drive me crazy sometimes, but I know you always do what you say you're going to do."

I considered all of this for a moment, then shrugged. "I suppose I could. It still seems a little weird to me, but if you need help, then I'm happy to help you. And I'd be happy to help out George as well. He definitely looks like he could use a little assistance. But what about my pie booth? I can't just leave all those pies sitting there while I drive George home."

"I'll pack up the pie shop for you," Grams said. "And I can watch Sprinkles all night if you want me to. I'm having a great time with him."

I looked over at her, surprised that she was so eager for me to drive George home. That's when I saw the mischievous glint in her eye. I knew what that meant: she wanted me to help Mitch, because she thought that would drag me into the case. Grams thought that I was the best amateur sleuth around. Whether she was right or wrong didn't matter. I had decided to swear off sleuthing. Grams thought that the last case had been dangerous, but I knew she thought I could handle this one from the fact that she'd just offered to close up the pie booth. I was about to protest when Molly piped in.

"Scott and I can also help clean up the pie booth, of course."

Mitch gave Molly a grateful smile, while I gave Molly a shocked look. Was she trying to get me back into sleuthing as well? I looked over at Theo, and he just shrugged. Apparently, he didn't see what the big deal was about any of this.

"Fine," I said. "If Grams and the others can close up my pie shop for me, I'll take George home."

Mitch leaned over and gave me a big hug, which felt strange since he still wasn't wearing a shirt. I ignored the way my heart flip-flopped in my chest, and tried to cover up my embarrassment by coughing. I didn't dare look at Theo, not wanting to see what his reaction to Mitch's hug would be.

"Well, the sooner the better," I managed to say. "Let me just grab my keys and purse from my pie booth, and I'll get George home right away."

That was how, about fifteen minutes later, after having witnessed a celebrity being murdered by a person in a monkey suit, I was driving toward one of the richest neighborhoods in Sunshine Springs with George Drake sobbing in my passenger seat. This was not at all how I had thought my first Sunshine Springs Fall Festival was going to go.

But I had a feeling deep down that the fun wasn't over yet.

CHAPTER FIVE

George Drake lived in the biggest house in the most expensive neighborhood in Sunshine Springs. It never ceased to amaze me how much wealth there was in this small, wine-country town. True, the majority of the residents lived a standard, middle-class existence—like myself and most of my friends. But there were quite a few people who had made their fortunes in the wine industry. Theo was probably still the richest man in town, and I was pretty sure his villa was bigger than George's house. But Theo's villa was a bit different since it was located on his winery grounds and not in an actual neighborhood. I did my best not to gawk as I pulled into the driveway that George indicated belonged to him.

Suddenly, I was glad that I had a brand new sports car. True, it was a much cheaper sports car than anything George ever would have driven. But at least it was new, and at least it was a "cool" car. It had been a bit of a splurge—a responsible splurge, but still a splurge. After my old car had been totaled in an unfortunate run-in with a tree, I'd decided that I deserved to upgrade my vehicle. I was trying to save money and keep my debt low, but I justified this one luxury by telling myself that it was important that I arrived in style when I made pie deliveries for the café. Really, I doubted anyone cared what sort of vehicle delivered their pie, but that was the story I told myself to keep from feeling guilty about not buying something more sensible.

And hey, you never knew when you'd randomly be chauffeuring around some filthy-rich passenger. I congratulated myself on having a car that wasn't completely embarrassing, and then I told myself to snap out of it and stop being so vain. George was staring straight ahead out my front windshield with a pitifully heartbroken expression on his face. I doubted he'd spent a single second thinking about what kind of car he was riding in. I cleared my throat, glad that he couldn't read my mind and see what ridiculous thoughts I was thinking.

"Well, here we are," I said brightly. "Try to get some rest. I know it will be hard, but it will be the best thing for you right now."

George balked at this. "You're not leaving me, are you?"

His eyes looked so full of anguish that I didn't have the heart to tell him that the last thing I wanted to do right now was spend any more time with him, or do anything else related to the terrible events of today.

Stifling back a sigh, I forced a smile onto my face. "If you'd like me to stay for a little bit, I can do that."

George's face brightened a bit. "Oh, would you? It's just been such a horrible day, and I can't bear the thought of being alone right now."

"I'd be happy to," I said, even though in reality I was dreading spending more time with him. As much as I didn't want to get wrapped up in all of this more than I already was, how could I leave poor George alone when he was clearly feeling so much distress? Besides, on the bright side, it would be interesting to see what the inside of his house looked like. I'd been inside Theo's villa several times, but other than that, I hadn't spent much time in rich people's homes. It always fascinated me to catch a glimpse of how the wealthy lived.

I followed George up the ornate stone footpath that led to his front door. The front door itself looked like a work of art. The windows in the door were made of stained glass, and you got the sense that you were about to enter a cathedral instead of a home. George must have noticed how mesmerized I was by the door, because he commented on it.

"You like it? I had it specially made. I spent some time living in France several years ago, and the beautiful cathedrals were always my favorite part. I wanted something that would remind me of them."

"It's beautiful," I murmured, gingerly reaching up to trace one of the windowpanes with my finger.

George nodded sadly. "Yes, so beautiful in fact that Big Al was planning to have one similar to it made for his new house in Sunshine Springs. But I guess that order will be canceled now." George's voice caught in his throat as he spoke, and I instinctively reached out to put a hand on his arm.

"This must all be such a shock for you. Let's go inside and sit down. Perhaps I can make you some tea."

George snorted as he unlocked and opened the front door. "Tea? I'm going to need something stronger than that. If you'd like to make me a whiskey, I would definitely be interested."

I wasn't sure that whiskey was the best thing for him right now, but I only smiled and nodded. After all, I couldn't judge people for their alcohol habits too much. Not when my café was named the Drunken Pie Café.

A few moments later we were inside, and I was doing my best not to gawk. While the outside had looked a bit like a French cathedral, the inside looked like a Greek palace. The floors were made of marble, and several floor-to-ceiling columns that looked like they belonged in an ancient temple were scattered around the open floor plan. In the living room, a purple velvet couch sat in front of a glass coffee table that was supported by golden legs. I wasn't sure I wanted to know whether the gold was real.

Massive paintings hung on the wall, but there didn't seem to be any real rhyme or reason to what had been hung where. Nothing seemed to match or flow, but all of it had obviously been framed in the priciest frames available.

I cast a sideways glance at George, who was heading toward a small bar in the corner of his living room, already searching for the whiskey. I wouldn't have pegged him as the overly showy type. He was dressed conservatively enough, although his shoes and jeans were obviously expensive. But, to be honest, the inside of his house looked downright tacky.

I resisted the urge to shake my head at his back, which was facing me now as he poured two glasses of whiskey. Some people had no idea what to do with their money. Theo's house was so tastefully decorated that it had never occurred to me that some people might not use their wealth in such a reasonable manner. George's house looked anything but reasonable. The only other home I'd seen from a truly rich man was the home of the late Edgar Bates, a wealthy citizen of Sunshine Springs whose murder I had investigated. But his home had been picked over by his gold-digging girlfriend before I saw it.

"Please, have a seat," George said, bringing me back to the present moment as he gestured toward his couch.

I was overcome by the sudden urge to run out the front door and away from all this craziness. Instead, I forced myself to smile once again, and made my way to sit on the velvet couch, which was surprisingly comfortable. At least it had function, even if it lacked form.

I didn't particularly want a whiskey right now. I generally only partook of whiskey when it was baked into one of my pies, and I couldn't remember the last time I drank it straight. But I didn't have the energy to decline George's attempt to be a good host, so I graciously took the glass and took a small sip. Hopefully, he wouldn't notice that I wasn't exactly guzzling it down.

He sat on the couch as well, but left plenty of space between us, which I had to admit gave me a sense of relief. A cynical part of me hadn't been able to help worrying that he was playing up his grief as a means to get me into his house to try to get cozy. He'd never given me any reason to think that he was that type of person, but I'd heard so many horror stories about wealthy bachelors that I couldn't help wondering if he'd only asked me inside in order to hit on me.

Hitting on me seemed to be the furthest thing from his mind right now, however. His eyes misted over once more, and he shook his head as he stared off into the distance.

"I just can't believe this," he said in a faraway voice. "It doesn't seem real. Everything was going so perfectly. After decades of not living in the same city as one of my best friends, Big Al and I were finally going to be together here in Sunshine Springs. I was going to help him invest here, and we were both going to grow old, fat and happy in this beautiful wine country. Then all of a sudden, poof! In just one moment, some crazy monkey took all of that from me."

"I'm very sorry," I said. I wasn't sure what else to say. What could one say to make things better in a situation like this? I was already feeling guilty that I'd been sitting here judging George for his taste in interior decorations. What business of mine was it how he decorated? If crazy paintings and a Greek temple vibe made him happy, then what right did I have to judge that? I mentally chided myself. I was here to help George, and I should put more of an effort into doing that if I was going to sit here and pretend to drink his whiskey.

"I'm glad that you at least had the last few months to spend a lot of time together and make memories," I said. "I know that doesn't take away the pain of losing him, but hopefully it at least gives you some small piece of comfort to hold onto."

A sob caught in George's throat again, and I chewed my lower lip. Perhaps that hadn't been the best thing to say? But I had no idea what the best thing was. At least I was trying. I looked uncomfortably over at George and saw that he was wiping tears from his eyes. But then, to my relief, he did crack a small smile.

"You're right," George said sadly. "We did have some good times together, both recently and in the years past. I should feel lucky that I had such a good friend. Not many people do, you know? I should be grateful for the time I did have."

Then, suddenly, he jumped up and set his whiskey glass down on the coffee table. He crossed over to a bookshelf across the room that looked like it was made of the same marble as the floors, and he ran his fingers over several leather spines until he found what he was looking for. He grabbed an armful of leather-bound volumes and brought them over.

"Here, I'll show you. These are photo albums from some of the good times Big Al and I had together."

He pushed the first leather photo album over to me and I opened it, almost afraid to touch it with my fingers that still felt covered in the grime, dirt, and pie that the day had brought. But George didn't seem disturbed by the sorry state of my fingers.

"Go on," he encouraged. "Open it."

I did as I was told, and found myself flipping through what looked like vintage photographs. A smiling, much younger George stared back at me from the pages. There were several photos of him in various theater productions, many of which Big Al had been in as well. There were plenty of people in the photos that I didn't know, but a young Big Al and a young George appeared frequently—often together, and always smiling and laughing.

"These are great," I said sincerely. "I had no idea you'd acted. Is that how you and Big Al met?"

"Yes," George said, smiling. "We were both in the same theater troupe when we were younger. He was always much more talented than I was, which probably doesn't come as a surprise since he's the one who went on to become a famous Hollywood actor. But we had some good times back in those theater days. We actually met when we auditioned for the same part in a musical. It was the lead role, and I got it, but Big Al was incredibly gracious about it. There were never any hard feelings, and he reached out to congratulate me and tell me he was looking forward to working with me. All that despite the fact that he'd been given merely a walk-on role." George smiled at the memory. "I never forgot his graciousness. And his hard work and good attitude paid off for him in the long run, as you know. Unfortunately, once he became famous, a lot of people screwed him over really badly." George sadly shook his head at this thought, pausing to take another long sip of his whiskey.

I felt my interest sparking. "Do you think one of those people might be the person who killed him?"

I didn't say the other things I was thinking: that Big Al seemed to have given a lot of people a reason to want to screw him over. He always acted so obnoxiously, and he definitely didn't come across as someone with good moral character. But I was sure George didn't want to hear that. Besides, what did I know? Perhaps Big Al had started out as a good person, and had grown bitter, obnoxious, and jaded after dealing with so many people who only cared about him because he'd become rich and famous. Perhaps George, as a longtime friend who had known Big Al before he'd stepped into Hollywood's bright lights, actually knew him better than anyone. Perhaps George had seen a side of Big Al that wasn't worthy of the judgments that so many of us in Sunshine Springs had so quickly passed on him.

George shook his head sadly. "I don't know. Over the years, many people have definitely decided that Big Al wasn't their favorite person. I'll admit that the more famous he became, the more he tended to push people away. But I can't blame him. He quickly learned that many were only after his money and the connections he could get them. But I still can't imagine who would have disliked him strongly enough to kill him. It just doesn't make sense. Would anyone really kill him just because he didn't give them the money they wanted? That seems a bit extreme, don't you think?"

I shrugged and nodded. It did seem extreme, but I had seen that money could be a strong motivator for murder. When someone was as wealthy as Big Al, you could never write off the possibility.

"Anyway," George said as he suddenly stood. "You look through those for a minute. If you'll excuse me, I'm going to run to the restroom."

I nodded absentmindedly and flipped through the albums as George disappeared to the bathroom.

Several of the albums contained pictures from vacations that Big Al and George had been on. In fact, the closer in time to the current day that the pictures became, the more they changed from acting photos to photos of Big Al and George on trips together, or hanging out around first Los Angeles and then San Francisco. There seemed to be big gaps in the years, though. As I went through the albums, there were spots where, from the looks of how much Big Al and George had aged in the photos, there must have been significant chunks of time missing here and there. Frowning, I stood and walked over to the bookshelf, wondering if some of the missing years were contained in other photo albums that George hadn't grabbed. I reached and pulled one down, and had just sat back down at the coffee table to look through it when George came back into the room. As he peered over my shoulder and saw what I was looking at, he made a bit of a strangled sound.

"Oh heavens! Don't look at that album! Those photos are so embarrassing!"

I glanced down at the photo on the first page. From the looks of it, this was another album of old theater photos. The picture on the first page was a shot of a group of actors that included Big Al and George. It didn't look like a formal photo, because everyone was casually dressed and even appeared to be goofing off a bit. I didn't see why anything like that would be so embarrassing, and I smiled up at George.

"Oh, come on. I've already seen plenty of old photos of you. What could possibly be so embarrassing?"

He groaned, and grabbed the album from me. "That was one of the worst acting jobs I ever did. I had actually landed a good role for once, but I botched it so badly! I don't know why I even keep this album. It just reminds me of that show. I forgot so many lines, and at one of the shows I even fell flat on my face. Of course, I don't blame myself for that entirely. The costume they made me wear was ridiculous. I probably wouldn't have tripped if I hadn't been wearing such a monstrosity."

I couldn't help but giggle. "Oh, come on. Let me see."

But George was adamant. He snatched the album away and shook a finger at me. "Nope. The only other person I know of that remembered that awful costume was Big Al. And I don't think he had any pictures of it. So now that he's gone, this is the only evidence of my most embarrassing days as an actor. I'll have to hide this away better, and no one will ever know that Sunshine Springs' most talented investor once fell flat on his face in the middle of a show."

He was trying to make a joke of things, but I could tell that he was genuinely embarrassed, and my heart went out to him a little bit. I guess even wealthy people had their insecurities. His face even turned a little bit red, although that could have been from the whiskey. George had already drained his glass, and he glanced at mine, which was still almost completely full since I'd only taken about three sips.

"Can I get you anything else?" George asked. "I'm sorry. I see whiskey isn't your thing. I should've asked." He poured a generous refill into his own whiskey glass and turned to give me a weary smile. "I'm usually a better host, I promise. It's just that I'm so exhausted today."

I stood, deciding that was my cue to leave. I'm not sure if that's what he intended by his words. In fact, I don't think it was at all. But I could see that he was tired and needed to rest. I was sure that he wasn't going to truly calm down until he had some time by himself, and he seemed in good enough shape now to be left alone.

Besides, I was more than ready to get home myself. "Thank you for the offer, but I'll pass. The whiskey is exquisite, truly. It's just that I don't feel much like drinking right now. I mostly feel like collapsing into bed, so, if you don't mind, I think I might go ahead and make my way home."

George did not argue with me. I got the sense that after I'd come inside, he'd regretted inviting me. He probably hadn't realized how tired he was until he'd sat down on his couch. Still, he managed to be unfailingly polite.

"Only if you're sure," he said. "You're welcome to stay as long as you'd like."

I smiled at him, impressed with his politeness. How had a man as nice as him ended up being friends with someone as obnoxious as Big Al? Maybe that was the thing, though. Maybe the fact that George was nice *was* the reason that he was friends with Big Al. As I stood and slung my purse over my shoulder in preparation to go, I couldn't help but wonder if perhaps George did know who might have disliked Big Al enough to murder him. True, he had said that he couldn't believe anyone would do this. But was that really true? If he really thought about it, perhaps he'd think of someone.

I told myself not to ask. I wasn't going to investigate this murder, and I was sure Mitch would be asking the question, so I didn't need to. But I couldn't deny that I had a burning curiosity, and, so far, George had seemed to be willing to talk about things. In fact, he seemed to feel better when he was talking. Telling myself that I was actually helping by asking about it, I couldn't resist.

"Are you sure you can't think of anyone that might have had motive to kill Big Al? Anyone at all? I know you said you can't believe someone would do that, but if you really think about it, there must be someone you suspect, since you knew him so well."

George squeezed his eyes shut for a few moments and rubbed his forehead. But when he opened his eyes again, he shook his head sadly.

"I just can't imagine who would actually do such a thing. I know Big Al wasn't perfect, and that he had his feuds. But I can't imagine who would hate him enough to do this."

My shoulders slumped. It seemed that George truly had no idea who the criminal might be. But then, as I once again started to turn toward the door, George spoke again.

"Well, there was that one thing… But, no. I just can't imagine…"

I turned with a frown. "Can't imagine what? What thing?"

George opened his mouth, but then promptly closed it again and shook his head. He shrugged at me. "It's probably nothing, and I don't want to speak badly about anyone here in Sunshine Springs without solid proof. We're a community, you know?"

I did know. But I also knew that George probably had a better sense of anyone about who might be guilty. I was about to push him on the topic, but at the last moment decided against it. If he had suspicions, he should tell them to Mitch, not to me. I was going too far by pressing him on the matter. He needed to rest, and I needed to rest. More than that, I needed to stay out of this murder case.

I mentally stamped out my curiosity and nodded at him. "I understand. But if you do think of someone that might be suspicious, you should definitely tell Mitch."

George nodded. "I know. But, to be honest, it's hard to talk to the police about this. Talking about it with them just makes it all seem so official." His voice broke as he spoke. "I just can't believe he's gone, and discussing his murder with law enforcement really makes it hit home what I've lost."

I wasn't a hugger by nature, especially with people I didn't know that well. But George looked so forlorn in that moment that I couldn't stop myself from crossing the room and giving him a big hug. When I pulled back, I was glad I had followed my instincts to hug him. It might have been just my imagination, but I could have sworn that he looked at least a little less sad.

"I know it's hard," I said. "But try to talk to Mitch. You'll have to talk to him eventually, and the sooner he has information, the easier it will be for him to find Big Al's killer. And Big Al deserves justice, don't you think?"

George nodded. "That he does. You're right. I'll talk to Mitch tomorrow. For now, I'm going to have this second whiskey and then go to bed. Thank you for everything, Izzy. It means a lot to me that you've cared so much, even when you didn't know Big Al personally. I'm sure if you'd had the chance to get to know him better, you would have really liked him, faults and all."

"I'm sure," I said with a kind smile, although I wasn't sure at all. Big Al didn't seem like the type of person I ever could have liked. But what harm did it do to agree with George now? There was no way I'd ever be expected to get to know Big Al now that he was gone. Besides, who knew? Maybe George was right. Maybe I, along with everyone else in town, had misjudged Big Al horribly. Perhaps if we had been given the chance to get to know him better, we would have realized that he wasn't all that bad. After all, Tiffany and Jenny liked him well enough.

Thinking of Tiffany and Jenny made me wonder if they had been questioned by Mitch yet. They had been closer to Big Al than anyone in town other than George. Had they had any clue that something like this might be coming?

But then, I shook my head and forced myself to stop thinking about it. Thinking about it was only going to drive me crazy, and I wanted to stay as far away from this as possible. Truly, I did. I bid George goodbye, and made my way out to my car without asking him any further questions.

When I got in my car and glanced down at my phone, I saw that Molly had texted me. She said that the festival was continuing on, and she and Scott had gone back to try to make the best of the day. She said that the community had actually rallied quite a bit, and that despite everything, the end of the festival was turning out to be quite a bit of fun. She wanted me to come join in on that fun.

She even told me that Grams had taken Sprinkles to the dance-off contest that was happening that evening. She texted me a video of Grams and Sprinkles on the dance floor. Grams was boogying down so low that I never would have believed how old she was if not for the fact that I had actually seen her birth certificate. And Sprinkles was having the time of his life, barking and spinning in circles as the music blared behind him.

I couldn't help but laugh. I was glad they were finding joy in the day still, but I knew that it was time for me to go home. I had a big day ahead of me at the pie shop the next day, since there would still be a lot of tourists in town, left over from the festival. I wanted to be ready to serve as much pie as possible and make as much money as possible, especially since I'd unexpectedly closed my booth early after Big Al's murder.

Not only that, but I also knew that going to the festival grounds and being near the scene of the crime would only make my detective instincts run on overdrive. It would be impossible for me to go to the festival without looking for clues or trying to decide who might have had a motive. I texted Molly a "thanks but no thanks" and told her to have fun, and then I revved my engine up and turned my car toward home.

CHAPTER SIX

I had known that the pie shop would be busy the day after the festival. But three days later, the place was still going crazy.

In fact, the whole town of Sunshine Springs was going crazy. I don't know why it hadn't occurred to me that the murder of a huge celebrity would suddenly put our town in the national spotlight, but now, it seemed so obvious.

Reporters had flooded in. They staked out every street corner, talking to everyone that passed by in hopes of getting some sort of inside scoop. It was a boon for local businesses, and usually I didn't complain about tourist dollars. But something just felt wrong about making so much money off of the fact that someone had been murdered. Still, what were we supposed to do? Shut down our businesses completely? That didn't make any sense.

And so I, along with everyone else, did my best to manage the unexpected wave of visitors. The Drunken Pie Café quickly became one of the most popular spots for the reporters, tourists, and heartbroken Big Al fans to visit. Word got out that it was a pie from my pie shop that had been smashed into Big Al's face right before he died, and for some morbid reason that made everyone want to try a piece of my pie. I supposed I should be grateful. It could have gone the other way, and people could have been avoiding my pie shop like the plague.

It also became well known that it had been the apple bourbon crumble that had been smashed into Big Al's face, and soon I couldn't bake enough apple bourbon crumbles to keep the masses happy. As I neared the end of the third day after Big Al had died, I was losing patience quickly.

I was exhausted, and I just didn't have it in me to answer any more questions for the legions coming through my door. I didn't know much about the murder case other than what had already made the rounds in the news. The only inside scoop I had was the little tidbit of George implying that he thought someone in particular in Sunshine Springs might have disliked Big Al enough to commit the murder. But I didn't know who exactly George had been referring to, and even if I had, I never would have told the masses. I wouldn't have wanted to reward the frenzied information seekers, and I wouldn't have betrayed George's trust like that.

I frowned at that thought. George actually hadn't trusted me. But I was just saying, if he *had*, I would have honored that trust.

As that third day wore on, I had started contemplating closing down the café early when I saw Scott walking into the pie shop. I always welcomed a visit from Scott, especially now that he was dating Molly and therefore didn't annoy me by flirting with me. He used to flirt with both of us, but obviously that had stopped since he and Molly became a thing. Now, his visits just meant the chance to chitchat with a friend, and possibly catch up on the town gossip.

Today, I wasn't sure I even cared about the gossip. I knew it would all be about Big Al's murder, and I was sick of hearing about the murder. But I *could* use the chance to talk to a friend.

As Scott entered with a package delivery in his hands, I motioned for him to go stand by the espresso machine. When the shop was super busy and I couldn't stop working completely to speak with him, I always had him hang out by the espresso machine. That way, I could talk to him while I made lattes or filled other drink orders. I had to admit that when Scott or Molly came in to talk to me, I often took my time even when I was just pouring glasses of wine, so that I would have a few moments with them. I didn't want to give the café's customers a bad experience, of course, so I never pushed my luck too much. No customer had complained yet, and sometimes you really did just need a few moments with a friend. Today was definitely one of those times.

Luckily, one of my customers ordered three lattes, so I had an excuse to stand by the espresso machine for several minutes.

"How are you holding up?" Scott asked. "And where is Sprinkles?

Hiding out in the back? I haven't seen him for a few days."

"Sprinkles is with Grams. She's been keeping him for me so he doesn't have to be cooped up hiding out from all these tourists."

On days that the café was busy, Sprinkles usually had to stay in the back office. Most of the Sunshine Springs locals didn't care if I gave him free run of the place, but the tourists tended to get irritated when they saw a dog wandering around. They would sometimes even make purposefully loud comments about how animals in restaurants were health hazards. I didn't want to deal with all of that, especially not on a crazy week like this one.

Scott nodded as he slid a package for me across the counter. "Good for him. I'm glad someone is escaping this madness, at least. And what's in this box, anyway? It's awfully light for such a large box."

I frowned at the box. "I'm not sure. I don't actually remember ordering anything, but that's not that surprising. My brain has been completely preoccupied with how crazy things around here have been."

"Tell me about it," Scott said. "It's been taking me twice as long as normal to finish my deliveries because I can't even drive down the street. All these crowds have descended on the town to see if they can spot any other celebrities coming through. A couple big Hollywood names have come to town, and you can always tell when they're around because the crowds start screeching the same way they used to screech when Big Al would walk by."

I wrinkled my nose. "Really? More celebrities are coming? Why? I would think they would have better things to do than see the spot where Big Al died."

Scott shrugged. "I would think so, too. But apparently not." He'd been keeping his voice relatively low, but he raised it a bit now as the milk frother on my espresso machine made it harder to hear—although he still didn't talk too loud. He didn't want anyone else in the shop to hear what he was saying. "Word on the street is that a lot of the celebrities are trying to act like they cared so much about Big Al because they think it's going to make them look popular and help them get parts in upcoming movies. I didn't think Big Al was even acting that much anymore, but apparently his untimely departure has left quite a hole in Hollywood's production schedule."

Scott shrugged, and I frowned as I finished frothing the milk.

"Why is everyone so intent on making a profit off of his death? The more I see the way the vultures are swooping in, the more I'm beginning to wonder who *didn't* have motive to kill him."

Scott nodded. "I know what you mean. It's gross. Speaking of motive, though: everyone in the media is saying that Bruce must have been the one to do this."

I raised an eyebrow. "Bruce Burnham?"

Scott nodded solemnly. "Yup. Some reporter latched onto the fact that Bruce had been in a feud with Big Al over the food poisoning thing, and the rest is history. Half the world is convinced that Bruce killed Big Al to get back at him for trying to bring down his restaurant. Ironically, this has made his restaurant more popular than ever. If there truly was food poisoning, I guess no one really cares."

I shook my head slowly, trying to take in this information. "But there's no way Bruce actually did it, is there? Yes, he was angry. But no one could blame him for that. That doesn't mean that he killed Big Al, and he just doesn't seem like the murdering type to me."

Scott shrugged. "He doesn't seem like the murdering type to me, either, but haven't you learned anything over the last several months? The idea that there's actually a murdering type is a bit of a fallacy. We've seen a few different murderers come through town, and I would say none of them exactly fit a certain profile."

I frowned as I considered this. I had finished the three lattes now and needed to take the next customer's order, but I didn't want to end my conversation with Scott just yet. "Can you stick around for a few minutes?" I asked him.

Scott laughed. "Why not? I'm hopelessly behind schedule thanks to all this traffic, anyway. Another few minutes won't change much."

I nodded gratefully, and went to take the next order, which thankfully was for a slice of pie and a latte. After getting the pie, I came back to the espresso machine to work on the latte—and to continue speaking with Scott.

"You know," I said, keeping my voice low. "Bruce never showed up at the crime scene, did he?"

Scott furrowed his brow. "No, I don't think he did. But that doesn't mean much. He could have been back at his restaurant booth. Or he could have been anywhere, really. Perhaps he didn't want to be around anywhere Big Al Martel was, even if the man was dead. Not everyone is such a glutton for gawking at crime scenes."

Apple Crumble Assault

I bit my lower lip as I frothed the milk for the latte, trying to think. Bruce had been quite angry at Big Al, and Scott was right. It didn't necessarily mean much to say that someone wasn't the murdering type. But still, I couldn't quite bring myself to believe that Bruce would actually kill Big Al. It seemed like an extreme reaction to what was probably a temporary bump in the road for his restaurant.

But if not him, then who? As far as I knew, there still hadn't been any big reveal of anyone with a motive strong enough to kill.

I shrugged my shoulders and tried to act like I didn't care. "Well, Mitch will figure it out, I'm sure."

Scott laughed. "You're a horrible actress, you know? It's so obvious that you can't stop thinking about this case."

I grinned sheepishly. "Well, you have to at least give me credit for trying. Besides, who in this town *isn't* thinking about it right now? It's impossible to go two seconds without seeing a reporter or overhearing a tourist talking about the murder scandal."

"True enough," Scott said. "It's a little too much gossip, even for me. And that's saying a lot."

"I know what you mean. Normally when there's gossip in town I make an appointment down at Sophia's Snips so I can stay up to date on the latest, but I don't even want to go near that place right now. I've had more than I can take just from what I hear in my pie shop every day."

Scott nodded. "Even Sophia herself has had enough. I heard she's thinking of closing down for a week and taking a vacation."

My eyes widened. Sophia Reed owned Sophia's Snips Salon and Spa, which was basically the only hair salon in Sunshine Springs. All the women in Sunshine Springs went there to get their hair cut, get facials, and get their nails done. As a bonus, anytime you had an appointment there, you were sure to hear the latest town gossip. Sophia loved to be at the center of things, so I was surprised to hear that everything had become too much even for her. I supposed that even a gossip-hungry town like Sunshine Springs had its limit—and we had all reached it.

I finished the latte and went to take another order. That customer asked for two glasses of wine, so I didn't have as much time to talk to Scott. Still, I poured it as slowly as I could.

"What about Tiffany and Jenny?" I asked. "Is anyone looking at them? They were involved in some sort of weird love triangle with him. Is it possible they know something about this?"

"I don't know," Scott said. "There's been a lot of news coverage of them crying their eyes out in grief over Big Al's death. To be honest, it's kind of obnoxious, because they're eating up the attention and enjoying being in the spotlight. You'd think they'd act a little more reverent after the supposed love of their life just died, but I suppose different folks grieve in different ways."

The tone in Scott's voice left no doubt that he didn't think eating up media attention was an appropriate way to grieve.

"Ugh," I said. "Well, I'm sure Mitch will be interviewing them, if he hasn't already."

"Yep," Scott said. "He must be really busy. Either that or he's in hiding. I haven't seen him at all since this whole thing started. I think he's trying to stay as far away from the reporters as he can."

I didn't blame him. "I should send a pie or two over to the station."

"I'm sure he'd appreciate that. Anyway, I should get going. Your line's not getting any shorter, and my packages aren't going to deliver themselves. Are you taking any days off this week?"

I shook my head sadly. "I don't think so. Things have been far too busy, and as you know I still don't have an employee." I groaned. "I don't know how I'm ever going to get an employee, since I'm always too busy to search for and hire one even though I desperately need one."

"Don't worry. I'm sure someone will turn up eventually. In the meantime, if there is a night this week that you still have energy after closing down the café, Molly and I would love to hang out with you for dinner."

I nodded. "I'd really like that. I'll keep you posted."

Scott took off, and I turned my attention back to the line at my front counter. But I had barely taken another order before the phone started ringing. I glanced over, intending to let it go to voicemail. I didn't like ignoring the phone, but I had to take care of the customers in my shop. Besides, a lot of the calls lately had been reporters wanting information on what had happened the day Big Al died. I didn't have time for that nonsense.

But when I glanced at the caller I.D. on the phone, I was surprised to see that the call was from the Sunshine Springs Police Station. My eyes widened in surprise, and I quickly snatched up the receiver. I had no idea why the police station was calling me, but I was sure there was an important reason for it. They had better things to do with their time right now than make social calls to the Drunken Pie Café.

"Hello?"

"Izzy! Thank God!"

I was even more surprised now: it was Mitch's voice on the line.

"Mitch? What's wrong?" I had a brief flashback to the last time Mitch had called me sounding this panicked. Then, he'd been calling because he'd been worried that someone was planning an attempt on my life. I couldn't help wondering whether that was the case again. My heart started pounding in my chest, and I looked nervously around the café, as though someone in there was just waiting to pounce on me. Nobody looked suspicious, but that didn't mean anything. Someone could be trying to fake me out.

Instead of answering me directly, Mitch danced around the question. He was good at doing that. "Can you come down to the station?"

"Now?" I asked, glancing around my pie shop once more. "I'm super busy down at the café…"

As much as I hated to shut down, I would do it if Mitch thought something was urgent.

"It doesn't have to be right this second if you absolutely can't get away, but the sooner the better. What time are you closing the pie shop tonight? I'll wait for you here as late as you want if you'll just come by."

I breathed out a little sigh of relief. Whatever this was, I knew it was important. Mitch wouldn't have called like this if it wasn't. But there was no immediate threat to my life. If there had been, he would have wanted me to come in immediately. Actually, come to think of it, he probably would have just driven down to the Drunken Pie Café himself instead of asking me to come in to the station.

It was odd for him to request that I come down, but I was sure there'd be a good reason for it. I was just glad that that reason didn't seem to be related to any danger on my life.

"Okay, I can probably be there by seven o'clock. Is that soon enough?"

There was a short pause on the line. "I hope so. I'll see you then."

I shivered as I hung up the phone, and wondered what news seven o'clock would bring.

CHAPTER SEVEN

I rushed through my closing duties at the Drunken Pie Café as quickly as possible that evening. Every minute of waiting until I could flip the sign on the door to "Closed" had been torture. I probably should have just done as Mitch asked and shut things down early, but I couldn't bring myself to turn away all that income. I'd spent my life's savings opening up this café, and I was desperately trying to rebuild those savings a bit before some financial disaster sank me.

This week had helped a lot with adding some cushion to my savings account, but it had also left me feeling like a giant ball of nerves. And Mitch's insistence on talking to me right away wasn't doing much to help calm those nerves.

I drove as fast as I could to the station, which wasn't very fast, since the traffic through Sunshine Springs' downtown area was still heavy from the evening dinner crowd. I shouted at several motorists who seemed to be more interested in sightseeing than in paying attention to green lights, but they ignored me for the most part. I grumbled loudly, suddenly wishing that I was driving to pick up Sprinkles instead of driving to the police station. I'd had enough of this week, and of all the crazy people who had descended on our normally calm little town.

But nothing prepared me for the level of crazy I encountered outside the police station. News vans were set up on nearly every available square foot of the parking lot, and several other cars I didn't recognize were parked out there as well. People toting giant cameras paced back and forth, and I had barely pulled into one of the few available parking spots when several eager faces appeared at my window.

"Good evening, ma'am," said a clean-shaven, slightly overweight man with a badge around his neck that proclaimed *Channel Seven Press Pass* in large, bold letters. "What is your business at the police station today? Have you come for something related to the Big Al Martel murder?"

For several moments, I just stared at him in disbelief.

I should have expected this, since the town was crawling with media. Why wouldn't they be camped outside the police station, where any murder suspects were bound to be brought? But somehow, in my worries over what Mitch was planning to tell me, it never crossed my mind that I would be facing a wall of news cameras just to get inside.

I knew better than to tell the reporters that I was there to see Mitch. Even though I didn't know why I was there to speak with him, I was sure they would press me on the issue and make up a salacious story about why I was at the station. I was also sure that wasn't what Mitch wanted, and more than that, I was sure that it wasn't what *I* wanted. Life was crazy enough at the moment as it was, with the town overrun by media, celebrities, and tourists. I had enough business at my pie shop to keep me busy without adding my face to the nightly news.

Thinking quickly, I got out of the car and reached into the back for some pie boxes. I often took leftover pie with me at the end of the day. Sometimes, I took some to Grams, sometimes I dropped some off at the library so the evening librarians could enjoy a delicious pick-me-up, and sometimes I just took the pies home and feasted on them myself. Hey, don't judge. I'm sure I burned a lot of calories being up on my feet all day at the café. I sometimes needed to replenish my energy.

But today, I was going to donate these pies to the Sunshine Springs police station, in the name of giving me a valid excuse to be there.

"I'm not here for anything related to the Big Al murder case," I said as I balanced the pie boxes in my arms. I closed the car door, hit the lock button on my key fob, and tried to push my way past the throng of reporters around me that was quickly growing thicker. These guys must have been at the station all day, and I doubted much exciting had happened. I knew Mitch well enough to know that he wasn't going to be interested in coming out here to update them. Besides, if anything exciting had indeed happened on the case today, I would have heard about it from Scott. No, it had been a relatively uneventful day, and that meant that these reporters had been sitting out here bored out of their minds. Some random lady with food boxes probably did seem exciting.

"Excuse me, please," I said sweetly. "I have a delivery. I need to get this food to the good officers inside. They're working so hard to keep Sunshine Springs safe, and they deserve sustenance."

When sweet talking didn't work. I resorted to pushing my way through the crowd of cameras, keeping my eyes lowered and hoping that no one would recognize that I was the owner of the Drunken Pie Café. I purposely hadn't mentioned that the food I was delivering was pie. If these reporters realized that I was from the café that had sold the pie to the monkey who smashed it in Big Al's face right before he died, I was sure these reporters would have a field day, asking me a thousand questions about that fateful day. I prayed that no one would recognize the Drunken Pie logo on the boxes, and hurried to the front door as quickly as possible—which wasn't all that quickly considering the throng that surrounded me.

I'd had several reporters come by the café this week fishing for information, and I'd said "no comment" about a thousand times the first day. After that, the reporters seemed to get the message that there was no story to be had from me. But if they realized who I was while I was here at the police station, they might think there was a story there after all.

Thankfully, after a few more moments of shoving my way through the crowd, I managed to get inside the front door. The receptionist had seen me coming, and had been standing just inside the door with it cracked open for me to slip through. She closed and locked it behind me, and I noticed that all the blinds in the windows were down and closed.

She shook her head at me in exasperation. "You're lucky I'm working late tonight so I could let you in. The news crews have been camped out there night and day since practically the moment of the murder. Mitch won't let them inside, and he won't speak to them. But that hasn't stopped them from hanging around like a pack of vultures waiting for a carcass to show up."

"You poor thing! It must have been an interesting couple days of work." Then I held up my armful of pie boxes. "But hopefully this will make it better."

The receptionist's eyes widened. "You realize there are just three of us at the station right now, right? We'll never be able to eat through an entire five pies!"

"I have faith in you. I'm sure you'll all put at least a good dent in the stack." I winked at her, and she laughed.

"Well, I appreciate the vote of confidence. You're here to see Mitch, right? He mentioned you were coming."

I nodded. "He wanted to talk to me about something, and apparently needed to do it in person. Quite mysterious." I wiggled one of my eyebrows, and the receptionist laughed.

"You know Mitch. He always has to keep an air of mystery around him. I don't know what he wants to talk to you about, but I know he's waiting for you. You know where his office is, right? You can show yourself back."

I nodded, then set the boxes of pie down on the large coffee table in the middle of the police station's reception area. I took one of the pie boxes for Mitch, and headed back toward his office.

I did indeed know where the office was. I'd spent quite a bit of time in there, considering I'd only lived in Sunshine Springs for a few months. But in that time, I'd managed to get wrapped up in several of Mitch's investigations, which tended to land me in his office in hot water.

This time, I'd been a good girl and had stayed out of everything, so I wasn't sure how I was ending up here again. I couldn't imagine that Mitch was angry with me, although who knew what rumors he might have heard through the gossip grapevine. Maybe someone had seen the reporters talking to me at the café earlier in the week and had assumed I was talking to them about the case. If that was all this was, I would reassure Mitch that I definitely wasn't trying to meddle in this case, give him the pie, and be on my way. I'd made a promise to stay out of things, and I intended to keep that promise. I really was trying to do better about not giving my friends cause to constantly worry about me, and Mitch was a good friend, even if he did drive me bananas on occasion.

But when Mitch opened his office door to my knock, he didn't look angry at the sight of me. In fact, he looked relieved.

"Izzy!" he exclaimed. Then he grabbed me by the upper arm, pulled me into his office, and slammed the door shut behind me as though worried that the reporters had somehow infiltrated the building and were going to follow me into his office. I'd never seen him looking quite so paranoid.

"Is everything okay?" I asked as I set down the box of pie on his desk.

"Everything's a mess." He went to sit in his chair, running his fingers through his hair and then cracking his knuckles loudly several times in a row. He didn't seem to even notice the pie box sitting on his desk, and that's when I knew that whatever this was, it was a really big deal. No matter how angry, worried, or generally upset Mitch was, I'd never seen him in a funk that couldn't be cured by one of my pies.

Until today.

I sat down across from him and nervously drummed my fingers on my knee, waiting for him to speak. He let out an agitated sigh, and finally noticed the pie. A half smile turned up the corner of one of his lips.

"I hope that's not apple bourbon crumble," he quipped.

I smiled back at him, relieved to see that his sense of humor was still intact. If Mitch hadn't been able to even manage a joke, the world would have pretty much been coming to an end. He always had a sarcastic remark about everything.

"Nope, the apple bourbon crumble has been selling out like crazy every day. For whatever morbid reason, everyone wants a taste of the pie that landed in Big Al's face moments before he died. This pie here is one of my death by chocolate pies, which, ironically, is actually the last pie Big Al ate before he died."

Mitch raised one eyebrow at me. "Ha. I don't think anyone actually mentioned that in any of the reports. But I guess that pie is appropriately named." He reached across his desk to pull the pie box closer. "I have to say, though, I'm willing to take my chances with this pie. Death by chocolate sounds preferable to death by media, which is what I feel is happening to me these days."

I glanced over my shoulder, as though I somehow could see through the walls of Mitch's office to the media circus beyond. I turned back to look at Mitch. "Surely they'll lose interest after a few more days."

Mitch picked up a plastic fork and loaded it directly from the pie without bothering to cut a piece. Instead of answering me directly, he merely grunted as he chewed.

I sat for a few more moments in silence, wondering what I was doing there. Perhaps he wanted a statement from me? I hadn't ever officially given one, even though I'd witnessed the whole murder. I'd figured if Mitch wanted one, he would have asked me for one. I also didn't think I would have much to add to what everyone else had already told him.

But if a statement was all he wanted, I still didn't understand why he'd been so strange about his request for me to come see him. He'd acted like it was urgent, and surely, a statement from me would not have suddenly become more urgent today than it had been any other day this week. I shifted uncomfortably in my seat, watching Mitch take bite after bite of pie as though he could chase away his frustration with death by chocolate. I tried to wait him out, but finally, my patience ran thin and I couldn't take it anymore.

"Are you going to tell me why you called me here, or are you just going to take out all your feelings on that pie?"

Mitch grunted, let out a long sigh, and then pushed back from his desk. He walked over to one of his filing cabinets and pulled out a large folder. He set the folder down in front of me without a word, then sat back down and started shoving more forkfuls of pie into his mouth.

"What's this?" I asked, staring doubtfully at the folder.

"Open it up and look."

Frowning slightly, I did as I was told. I found that inside the folder were several newspapers, as well as printouts from online news articles. As I flipped through, it appeared that the newspapers came from not only local areas, but also from across the nation. I saw papers from major cities in California like San Francisco and Los Angeles, and even blips from national papers like the *New York Times* and the *Washington Post*. It appeared that all of the articles in the folder had to do with Big Al Martel's death. I shouldn't have been surprised that it was making national headlines. National news media had been crawling around our little town all week, and Big Al Martel had been quite popular. Still, it felt a little dizzying to sit there and stare at a stack of articles all about my hometown and the murder that had occurred here last weekend.

As I started to flip through the articles, I soon realized why Mitch was acting so grumpy—or, at least, *one* of the reasons he was acting so grumpy. I wasn't sure how many things, exactly, were bothering him right now. I would say quite a few from the way he was going at that pie, but perhaps the biggest thing was sitting there in black and white right in front of me: several of the articles had photos of the crime scene. With all of the tourists and Big Al fans that had been crowding around with their cell phones, it was no surprise that plenty of photos existed of the aftermath of the stabbing.

And, plenty of photos existed of Mitch in his wrestling costume.

As I flipped through the articles, I saw several with headlines such as "Sunshine Springs Police Chief Too Busy Playing Dress-up to Stop a Murder." There were several articles that mentioned that Mitch was not giving any comments on the ongoing investigation, and many journalists had theorized that this was because he didn't know what he was doing, or because he was too busy wrestling to spend time tracking down Big Al's murderer. I knew that Mitch never commented on investigations, but of course the media would spin things however they wanted.

"Wow," I said as I flipped through the articles. I didn't know what else to say. There were a lot of different pictures of the crime scene from many different angles, but the majority of them had Mitch in there wearing his ridiculous wrestling outfit, holding up his sheriff's badge, and looking at the crowd with an angry grimace on his face.

Mitch sighed. "As you can see, my costume made national news. I wonder if that means I should automatically be considered the winner of this year's costume contest, which was never actually completed after the murder."

I looked up at Mitch, and even though I knew it was the wrong thing to do, I couldn't hold back a snort of laughter.

He looked up from the pie and glared at me. "You think this is funny, Izzy? And anyway, is this really the first time you're seeing these? Every news outlet everywhere seems to think it's hilarious to broadcast pictures of me in that costume. They're making me look like a clown because I was participating in a community event. How was I supposed to know that there would be a murder in my village before the costume contest even started?"

I shrugged at him. "I haven't seen any of this until just now. I've been too busy at the café to pay much attention to the news, and, to be honest, I haven't really wanted to see what the media is saying about our little town. They've been rude enough to me when they came into the café that I had a feeling it wasn't anything good. Still, you have to admit this is pretty funny."

I tapped a finger on one of the pictures.

Mitch gave me a death stare. "It's not funny. What it is, is a mess."

I nodded contritely, not sure what else to do. I did think it was rather funny to see Mitch in the national news in a wrestling singlet, but I could certainly see that he might have a different view of the matter. I felt a little badly, and tried to speak in a more sympathetic tone.

"I'm sure this must all be really frustrating. Is there any way I can help? Hopefully it at least makes you feel a bit better to know that I haven't seen anything. There must be other people in town who are too busy to have noticed as well. Oddly enough, this whole situation has been quite a business boom for all of us."

Mitch rubbed his forehead, took a deep breath, and opened his mouth to speak. But then, he shut it again. He ate a few more bites of pie, and the agitated look on his face only increased. Clearly, he wanted to tell me something, but he was hesitant to do so for some reason.

"Mitch," I said gently. "Whatever it is you want to say, just spit it out. We're good friends. If there's something I can help with, just ask."

Mitch sat back and sighed. "I do need your help. But the thing is, I'm not sure it's fair of me to ask for it."

"Why not? That's what friends are for: to help each other out in any way they can."

Mitch nodded, looking miserable. "I know. But the thing is, I can't get any investigating done on this case. The media are gleefully trying to get any pictures they can of me. I've become some sort of weird human interest story because of that stupid wrestling costume. Besides that, just the fact that they know that I'm the Sheriff means they follow me everywhere in hopes of being the first to break some big piece of news regarding Big Al's murder. The way things are going, this case will never be solved. I can't step two feet outside this office without being mobbed."

"I could see that," I said slowly, thinking of all the news vans sitting in front of the police station. "But how can I help with that?"

Mitch looked up at me with a sheepish expression on his face. "You could take over the investigation for me."

For several long moments, all I could do was stare at Mitch. My jaw dropped, and silence hung so thickly in the room that I felt it was literally weighing me down.

When I did find my voice, I could barely do more than stammer. "But...but...you always tell me to stay out of things."

Mitch nodded, already looking like he was feeling a bit better just to have gotten that off his chest. "I know I've told you to stay out of things. But you *are* a good detective. I've admitted that before. And right now, nobody really knows who you are. Sure, a few people have realized that you're the owner of the Drunken Pie Café, but no one expects you to be investigating this. They won't think much of you wandering around town looking for clues. They won't even realize that you're looking for clues."

I still sat there in shock. "But you always tell me it's too dangerous to chase after murderers. Why would this case be any less dangerous than any of the others?"

Mitch chewed his lower lip, looking conflicted. "I know what I said. But I honestly don't think this case is that dangerous. Whoever this murderer was, they clearly had a vendetta against Big Al. I doubt they're going to think much of a pie shop owner wandering around. Besides, I'll give you plenty of protection. I can give you some undercover bodyguards, and I'll have my officers watch you from a reasonable distance."

I waved him away. "I don't need bodyguards. It doesn't scare me to work on these cases, and I only agreed to stop because you wanted me to. But now you're telling me that you've changed your mind."

Mitch looked pained. "It's not that I don't care about you, or that I don't think it's a lot to ask. It's just that..."

Mitch trailed off, apparently unsure of what to say. Then he shook his head, and stood to start gathering up the news articles and put them back in the folder.

"You know what, never mind. I shouldn't have asked. It's not fair of me."

I stood as well, and put a hand over Mitch's hand, stopping him from putting the papers away. He looked up at me, pain and anguish in his eyes. Then he looked down at our hands, and I suddenly realized that it was a bit awkward that I was basically holding his hand. I drew my hand away, but I kept looking into his eyes.

"I'll help you. I don't mind. And despite what you think, I know how to be careful. To be honest, I've been trying my best not to think about this case, but I haven't been able to get it out of my head. I'd love the chance to try to solve it."

Undeniable relief washed over Mitch's face. But before he could speak, I held up my hand.

"The only thing is that my café is extremely busy right now. I'll do what I can, but I'm not sure how much time I'll be able to devote to this."

Mitch nodded. "I know. I'm not expecting you to sacrifice your café for this. In fact, I've already talked with one of my officers and asked if he'd be willing to work at your café during the investigation. I'll pay him to work there, and I'll pay you for your work on the investigation. I don't care what it takes. I just need your help with this, and I need to get the case squared away so that Sunshine Springs can get back to normal once again."

I smiled at him. "Alright then. I'll do it. I actually have a few ideas about how to investigate this…"

Mitch laughed. "Of course you do. I know you: even though you told me that you weren't going to investigate—and I do believe that you've been trying to stay out of things—you can't turn your mind off, can you?"

I looked at him sheepishly. "I guess not."

He smiled. "At least if you're investigating with my blessing I can keep better tabs on you and make sure you're safe. I can also give you this."

He opened a closed cabinet on one of his bookshelves and pulled out a heavy vest and a radio. I raised an eyebrow, and he shrugged. "This is a bulletproof vest. I'd appreciate it if you'd wear it when you're out investigating. It's probably overkill, but it would make me feel better. And here's a radio. If you hit this red emergency button, it will broadcast an emergency signal and your location to the entire Sunshine Springs Police Department. Don't hesitate to use it if you feel you're at all in danger."

I nodded, and took the vest and radio from him. I could hardly believe this was happening. I'd never thought I would see the day that Mitch would condone my working on a murder investigation, especially after I had sworn off of sleuthing for good. But here I was, being told to go for it.

"Oh, one more thing." Mitch went back to his file cabinet and pulled out another thick folder. "This is a copy of the case notes. Whatever small clues we already have are in here. I'll be honest, though: there isn't much. But maybe something will point you in the right direction."

I tried not to smile too giddily. I couldn't believe that I was holding the official case reports in my hand. Today felt like Christmas.

I decided it was time to get out of there before Mitch changed his mind. I could tell that he still wasn't sure about sending me off into the wild to chase down a murderer, and I didn't want him to tell me to forget about it.

I glanced toward the door, then looked around the office. "Do you have a bag I can put this all in? I should keep this stuff hidden, or the media's going to wonder why I'm carrying a bulletproof vest, a police radio, and a police file out with me."

Mitch nodded. "Good point. I actually have the perfect bag for you."

He reached into one of his cabinets again and pulled out a large tote bag with the Drunken Pie Café logo on it. I'd ordered a bunch of totes when I first opened my café, but they hadn't turned out to be very practical for hauling pies around. I'd given most of them away, and had since forgotten about them. But now, this tote would be the perfect way for me to hide everything Mitch had given me. I shoved the vest, the radio and the file into the bag and slung it over my shoulder. Then, I rushed toward the doorway.

"I should get going before everyone wonders why it's taking me so long to deliver food," I said, hoping Mitch wouldn't think it was strange that I was trying to bolt so quickly.

Mitch nodded, but put a hand on my shoulder to stop me. I spun around to look at him, holding my breath and worrying that he was going to tell me he'd changed his mind and that he couldn't live with himself if anything happened to me. But he didn't say that. Instead, he looked so deeply into my eyes that I squirmed uncomfortably under his gaze.

"Thank you, Izzy. Really. I don't feel I deserve your help after the way I've yelled at you to stay out of things before, but I really do appreciate it. I'm at my wits' end here, and I just want things in

Sunshine Springs to get back to normal."

I smiled at him, trying to ignore the way that my heart did a flip-flop when he looked at me that way with those blue eyes of his.

"It's no problem, really. I'm happy to help. Now try to relax a little and eat that pie. I'll keep you posted on what I discover."

Then, I turned and made a beeline out of the station and straight to my car. A few of the reporters tried to ask me if I'd seen anything interesting inside the station, but I ignored them. They didn't push me too hard for a comment. They must have figured that I probably hadn't learned much during a food delivery.

Oh, how wrong they were about that.

I couldn't keep a stupid grin off my face as I revved my car up and drove away from the police station. I felt elated that my sleuthing days weren't over, after all, and I could hardly wait to get home and dive into the case file Mitch had given me. I intended to read it as soon as possible, just in case he changed his mind and told me to let him take over again. Now that I was letting myself think about the case, I couldn't hold back my excitement.

"Watch out," I whispered to whomever Big Al's murderer was, even though they obviously couldn't hear me. "Izzy James is coming for you."

CHAPTER EIGHT

After leaving the station, I drove by Grams' house and picked up Sprinkles. I didn't tell her that Mitch had put me on the case. Ordinarily, I told Grams everything. But right now, I was worried that if I said anything about this, I would ruin my good luck. Call me superstitious, but I didn't want to jinx myself.

As soon as I got home, I fed Sprinkles, who was in a huff that I didn't have any pie for him. I apologized half-heartedly, but I knew he'd get over it.

"Sorry, boy. I had to sacrifice all the extra pie today in order to get into the police station. It turns out I've got a new case to work on."

I beamed at him, and he looked back at me skeptically. I wasn't sure how much of what I was saying he understood, but I figured it must be a lot. I wondered if he was thinking about how I'd nearly been killed in the last case. I might have been dead if it hadn't been for his running to get help on my behalf.

"This isn't going to be as dangerous, I promise. Mitch is going to have his officers keep an eye out for me, and besides, I've got a bulletproof vest. Look at this!"

I held up the vest, and Sprinkles whined. The fact that I had it didn't seem to make him feel any more secure.

I shrugged, set the vest aside, and went to start reviewing the case file Mitch had given me. My excitement was tempered a bit when I opened the file and saw how meager the clues Mitch had really were. He'd interviewed the suspects that I would have expected. Bruce—the owner of the Spicy Grape Restaurant, and the one who had been feuding with Big Al over the food poisoning incident—had been interviewed.

From the transcript, it sounded like Bruce had been quite belligerent during the interview. He'd said he hated Big Al but wouldn't have killed him, although he understood why someone would have. He'd also ranted for quite some time that Big Al had gotten what was coming to him. Bruce hadn't seemed at all worried that his angry comments might make him look more suspicious. I wasn't sure whether that spoke more to his innocence or guilt, but after reading the transcript over a few times, I had to admit that there was nothing in there that seemed particularly earth-shattering. It was no secret in Sunshine Springs that Bruce hated Big Al, and even in the wake of Big Al's death, Bruce didn't seem shy about reiterating that fact.

Of course, in addition to interviewing Bruce, Mitch had had his officers search Bruce's restaurant and home. But according to the report I held in my hands, nothing had been found to indicate that Bruce might have been the murderer: no monkey costume, no receipts for the purchase of any monkey costume, no knives that had the remains of Big Al's blood on them...nothing of interest.

The lack of evidence didn't conclusively prove that Bruce was innocent. He could very well have hidden everything away somewhere far from his home or restaurant. That's what any smart murderer would have done. But for the moment, Bruce was a dead-end.

I wasn't going to write him off completely, and Mitch hadn't either from the looks of the case file. There were several notes about how Bruce still had the strongest motive of anyone. But motive alone wasn't enough. If Bruce was to be arrested for this murder, there would have to be some sort of actual proof. As of yet, there was none. Whether that would change in the future or not, who could say?

On a small notepad, I wrote *Bruce?* and left it at that for the moment. I would investigate him further, but first I wanted to see what else was in the case file.

Tiffany and Jenny had also been interviewed, but their transcripts were even more of a rambling mess than Bruce's. They each blamed each other for Big Al's death. Both of them ranted at some length about how Big Al had been the love of their lives and had been taken from them.

Tiffany claimed Jenny killed him to spite her, and Jenny claimed Tiffany killed him to spite her. Neither of them had any proof, and a search of their homes turned up plenty of Big Al paraphernalia, but didn't find anything actually related to the murder. On my notepad, I wrote *Tiffany? Jenny? Love triangle gone bad?*

Then I looked up and sighed. Mitch really hadn't found much. No wonder he was so frustrated. The rest of the case file consisted of interviews with people who had been at the scene of the murder, but it didn't sound like anyone knew anything more than I did. Plenty of people had seen the monkey stab Big Al, but the costume had been so good that no one had any clue who the monkey was. And, unfortunately, everyone had been in such shock right after the stabbing that the monkey had easily gotten away.

To my amusement, there was an actual photo of the exact moment the monkey had pied Big Al—and the photo came from Molly. Molly had taken a selfie right as the monkey had launched the pie. She'd turned in the selfie to Mitch, but the monkey costume didn't show any indication of who was underneath it. The monkey did look rather tall in the selfie, but who was to say that wasn't a trick? It could be that the monkey was a tall man, like Bruce. Or it could be that the monkey was wearing platform shoes to disguise its true height, and was actually someone shorter, like Tiffany or Jenny.

I shook my head in frustration. Surprisingly, there were no other photos of the monkey. There were a few photos of Big Al with pie in his face, but somehow, nobody except Molly had captured the actual monkey. Everyone had been too focused on Big Al to worry about a monkey, who, until the moment of the stabbing, had been just another costume in a crowd full of several costumed characters.

In frustration, I paged through the file again, but looking at everything once more didn't reveal any new clues. I really did have my work cut out for me if I was going to solve this case. I tapped my pen on my notepad and tried to decide what to do next. One idea I had was to talk to George. He'd had a suspicion of who might be guilty, but he'd also seemed pretty adamant that he didn't want to talk about it.

I wasn't sure I wanted to push him too hard at this exact moment. Perhaps if he had a few days to grieve and come to terms with the shock of what had happened, then he'd be more willing to talk. There wasn't an interview from him in the case file yet, although I was sure that Mitch had requested one. My guess was that Mitch was giving him space for a few days, and if Mitch was doing that, I figured I should too. Mitch wasn't the type to give space unless he really thought it was necessary, so I would follow his lead on that.

I made a note on my notepad to contact George after another day or two. For the moment though, what should I do? I needed to start my investigation by talking to Bruce, Tiffany, or Jenny. But which one?

I stared at their names on my notepad, and finally decided that investigating Bruce would be my best bet. As crazy as Tiffany and Jenny were, I couldn't quite see them actually pulling off a murder. They seemed a bit too ditzy to accomplish something that required so much careful and clever planning. Of course, the ditzy thing could have been an act, but still. Bruce appeared to be the likeliest suspect. It was a bit hard for me to imagine him actually killing someone, but I had seen how angry he was at Big Al. Perhaps I would do well not to underestimate that anger.

Of course, I didn't think Bruce would be too excited to talk to me if I marched up to him and told him I was investigating the murder. I decided that the fact that he didn't know I was sleuthing would serve me well here, and I thought I knew just the way to get up close to him without raising his suspicion.

With a small smile on my face, I picked up my cell phone and dialed Theo's number.

"Izzy?" Theo asked before even saying hello. He sounded like he was in the middle of some sort of giant party.

"Yeah, it's me. What are you doing? Sounds like you're at a rave."

Theo groaned loudly into the phone. "No, not a rave. I'm hosting a private event at the winery's tasting room tonight. Some of the celebrities that came into town asked if they could rent out the facility for the evening. They offered me enough money that I wasn't going to turn it down, but now I'm regretting it. There's not enough money in the world to make me put up with this kind of chaos. Celebrities are a bit crazy. I don't suppose you want to come down here and keep me company, do you?"

"No, sorry. Wild celebrity parties aren't my thing. But I did call to see if you want to hang out."

"Oh?" Theo sounded surprised.

Usually, he was the one inviting me to hang out. It's not that I didn't like spending time with him. It's just that I always worried that if I invited him to do anything, that he would take it the wrong way and think I was interested in him romantically. He was always looking for the slightest sliver of hope that I might want to date him.

Which meant that I was treading on dangerous ground with what I was about to ask. But it couldn't be helped. I needed to go to Bruce's restaurant, and it was too fancy of a place to casually go in on my own. I would raise suspicions if I didn't have a friend or a date with me.

"I'm planning to go to the Spicy Grape tomorrow," I said to Theo. "Want to come with me? Strictly as friends, of course. But I'm helping Mitch a little bit with the investigation into Big Al's murder, and I thought going to the restaurant might be a good way to get my bearings in the case and see if I can find out anything about Bruce."

Theo didn't speak for several moments, during which time I could hear the shouting and raucous laughter in the background. Finally, he asked, "You're helping Mitch? Does *Mitch* know about this? I thought you weren't sleuthing anymore."

"Mitch knows," I said proudly. "He actually asked me to help."

"He did?" Theo sounded surprised, and I was a bit surprised that Mitch hadn't told him. The two of them were best friends, and I would have assumed Mitch would have told Theo that he was breaking down to ask for my help. But perhaps they hadn't had a chance to talk. Theo had probably been as busy as I was given how many celebrities and tourists were hanging around because of Big Al's murder. And Mitch had been hiding out. He probably hadn't seen Theo in the last several days.

"It's a bit of a long story," I said. "But if you want to come to the Spicy Grape with me tomorrow night, I'll explain everything."

There was another pause as Theo considered this information. Then, he chuckled. "Okay. Just when I think this week can't get any stranger, Mitch actually tells you to do some detective work, and you call me up to go on a date."

His voice was teasing, and I knew he was just trying to rile me up, but I still felt the need to set him straight.

"It's not a date. It's just a friends' thing. I need someone to come with me to the restaurant, and it would be a little weird if I went with Scott and Molly because the Spicy Grape isn't exactly a love triangle kind of place. It's not where you take your third wheel friends."

"Is that what you feel like with Scott and Molly? The third wheel? They seem like they're trying to do a good job of including you."

I shrugged, even though Theo couldn't see me. "Oh, they do a great job of including me. But I think it would just look weird to be a threesome at the Spicy Grape."

"So instead of looking like a third wheel, you're going to go on a pretend date with me."

"Not a pretend date exactly. Just a 'let's hang out as friends and if someone assumes then we'll let them' sort of thing?"

Theo laughed. "You're ridiculous. But I'd love the chance to hang out with you, and I do love the Spicy Grape. So yes, I'll go on a 'non-date' date with you tomorrow to help you investigate the murder, since apparently the world has turned on its head and Mitch is condoning this now. I can't wait to hear how this all happened."

I smiled. "It's not that exciting of a story, but I'll tell it to you anyway. And I am hoping that things will start to get a little more exciting as I look into this case."

"Hopefully not *too* exciting," Theo said. "The last case you worked on involved so much excitement that you nearly got killed. But I'm going to assume that Mitch wouldn't put you on this case if he thought that was going to happen again."

"No, he wouldn't," I said. "See you tomorrow, then?"

"Yep, sure thing. Text me the time once you get a reservation. For now, I have to go. This group is harder to supervise than a gang of belligerent teenagers." I heard a huge crash in the background, and Theo groaned. "Okay, really gotta go. See you tomorrow."

He ended the call, leaving me in sudden silence. I smiled, and shook my head, feeling lucky to be such good friends with him. Life was never boring with Theo around.

I picked up the phone again to dial the Spicy Grape for a reservation. But as I waited for someone to answer, I couldn't help thinking about what Theo had said. I did hope that things wouldn't get *too* crazy on this case. Surely, Theo was right. Mitch wouldn't put me on this case if he thought things were going to get too dicey.

Nevertheless, I shivered as I realized that the person behind the monkey costume could be anyone, and that they might not be too happy if they realized I was trying to find out who they were. I hoped that my little "date" with Theo tomorrow would set me on the path toward figuring this out sooner rather than later.

CHAPTER NINE

I insisted on driving myself to the Spicy Grape. I worried that if I let Theo pick me up, he would consider it too much like a date. I was determined to keep this firmly in friends territory. And what were friends for if not for helping each other solve a murder case?

When I arrived at the restaurant, I was surprised at how full the parking lot was. There were hardly any spaces available, and I felt lucky that I'd even been able to get a reservation. It looked like business was booming once again.

Before Big Al's murder, Bruce's restaurant had taken a huge hit from the food poisoning incident. Even though Sunshine Springs residents were usually loyal to their own, Big Al had made such a big deal out of it that many in Sunshine Springs had been hesitant to eat there, just in case. Not only that, but most tourists had been more than a little hesitant to visit the place, and tourists made up a big portion of the restaurant's clientele.

But, apparently, there's nothing like a murder to get people going to a restaurant once again. There were even a few news vans parked outside, although thankfully the bored-looking reporters barely acknowledged me as I climbed out of my car. If they did know that I was the owner of the pie shop from which the pie in Big Al's face had come, they didn't care. That was old news by now, and I'd made it clear that I had nothing further to say about it. For all they knew, I was just coming here for a nice dinner, completely unrelated to anything having to do with Big Al and his murder.

Oh, how wrong they were.

I got out of my car and walked toward the restaurant, feeling a bit self-conscious in my formfitting royal blue dress and leather knee-high boots. It wasn't often that I dressed up, and even though I'd taken pains to make sure that this wouldn't be considered a date, I couldn't help feeling nervous thinking about what Theo would say when he saw me.

I'd also done my hair and put on makeup, and that wasn't something I did every day. At the café, I tended to have my hair up in a bun, which was a messy bun by the end of the day whether I had intended that look or not. I also rarely wore full makeup. What was the point, when it would just be sweated off my face by the end of the day? At most, I tended to put on lip gloss and do my best to remember to reapply it. Luckily, I'd been blessed with the same good skin that Grams had, and I didn't look completely frightening without makeup on.

Now, I was beginning to wonder if I should have just left the makeup off tonight as well. Was Theo going to take me seriously about this not being a date when I'd made such an effort to dress up? And, more importantly, *why* had I made such an effort to dress up? Was I more interested in impressing Theo than I'd admitted even to myself?

I shook my head as if to shake these thoughts away. I told myself that I was dressed up because I was coming to the Spicy Grape, and the Spicy Grape was known as a fancy place. That's what you did when you went to a fancy restaurant, right? You dressed up. Especially when you were trying to fit in so that no one would suspect that you were actually there to try to dig up clues about a murder case.

A low whistle as I entered the restaurant told me that my outfit had definitely impressed Theo. I bit my lower lip and tried to keep from smiling as I met his eyes. Of course he was here ahead of me. He would never take the chance on letting a lady arrive before him, even if that lady refused to allow him to drive her to dinner.

"You clean up nice," he said. "It's been a minute since I've seen you in anything but a Drunken Pie apron. Not that you don't look amazing in an apron, either. But this, this…" He gestured toward me, making a motion to encompass all of me with his hand. "This is just incredible. I'm going to have to call Mitch to arrest you, because looking this good should be a crime."

I rolled my eyes at him. "You're so cheesy. Who actually says stuff like that in real life?"

Theo grinned and shrugged. "Me?"

Then, he reached out and offered me a hand. "Shall we?"

For a moment, I consider declining his hand. After all, if this wasn't a real date, why would I walk into the dining room holding his hand?

But there was a small part of me that really wanted to let him hold my hand. I justified it by telling myself that we needed to maintain a good cover so that no one would suspect why I was really there.

Deep down, I knew that was just the story I was telling myself. The truth was that even though I wasn't ready for a relationship, and wasn't sure when I would be, Theo Russo was an addiction I couldn't quite shake. I had almost kissed him once, under an orange tree in the shade of his magnificent villa. It had been a picture-perfect moment until we'd been interrupted by Mitch and a gang of his officers, who were hot on the trail of solving a murder. Even though I knew Theo would repeat that moment in a heartbeat, I had rebuffed him. But I couldn't help wondering what might have happened if Mitch hadn't interrupted us on that fateful day.

I tried my best not to let Theo's handsome looks and charming personality get to me, but in moments like this, it was hard. He was wearing a full suit and a crisp, emerald green tie that brought out the green notes in his deep brown eyes. He walked with confidence, the way you'd expect a successful businessman like him to walk, and I couldn't help but notice that heads turned as we followed the hostess into the dining room a few moments later. I knew that if any of the Sunshine Springs locals saw us, they would be whispering around town that Theo and I had been on a date. But for once, I didn't mind being part of the rumor mill. Was it really so bad if people assumed that Theo and I were an item?

We weren't, of course, but who cared what people thought? Could I really complain about being associated with one of Sunshine Springs' wealthiest, most popular residents?

I mentally kicked myself as I sat down at the table. What was I doing? I was here to work on a murder case, not to daydream about Theo. Maybe I should have just come here with Scott and Molly after all, third wheel or not.

We had barely been seated when our waiter approached us,

seeming slightly nervous. "Mr. Russo, so good to see you. I'm assuming you'd like some wine?" The waiter laughed nervously at his own joke. Theo kindly grinned at him and played along.

"We would indeed like some wine. I hear you have a few decent bottles from some little-known winery called the Sunshine Springs Winery? Perhaps you have something that's at least drinkable from them? I know that's a tall order, but let's see what you can do."

The waiter chuckled, pleased that Theo seemed to have enjoyed his joke. "We're recommending the 2016 Pinot tonight. Does that sound alright for you?"

Theo smiled. "Of course. That's one of my winery's best vintages. I'd love a bottle of it."

The waiter scampered off to get the wine, and I looked at Theo and shook my head. "It must be so strange to be such a local celebrity."

It wasn't the first time I'd said something like this to Theo, but sometimes I still couldn't quite wrap my head around it. Everyone knew everyone in a town like Sunshine Springs, but Theo was known on a whole different level. He was respected and revered as the owner of the winery that had put Sunshine Springs on the map. Yet through it all, he managed to somehow remain humble and kind.

And through it all, he somehow was interested in me—even though he could have had pretty much any single woman he wanted in Sunshine Springs.

I mentally kicked myself again. There I went, thinking about never-gonna-happen romances when I was supposed to be thinking about Big Al's murder.

Theo shrugged at me. "I guess it's hard to take all the praise of me seriously when it was my dad who really built the winery up. I just took it over from him, and I hope I'm doing a good job with it. But all the credit belongs to him."

Our waiter came back then, cutting our conversation short. He opened the wine and poured us both glasses, then read off the specials of the day. "I'll give you both a moment to decide. But let me know if you have any questions."

I figured this was as good a time as any to open up the subject of Bruce. I glanced around, making sure no tourists or media were close enough to hear me, and then dove right in.

"Actually," I said in a low voice. "I do have a question. "How is everyone holding up around here after Big Al's murder? I heard the police talked to Bruce and searched the place."

I saw a flicker of uncertainty in the waiter's face. He glanced backward over his shoulder as if worried someone was going to hear him talking, and I felt disappointment rising within me. I had asked too soon. I should have waited a bit and tried to win his trust before jumping right in with questions.

But luckily, Theo seemed to know just how to smooth over the situation. He lowered his voice into a conspiratorial tone and spoke to the waiter as though they were best friends sharing a secret.

"Between you and me," Theo said, "I'm glad to see that the murder hasn't hurt Bruce's business. We need a good, strong tourist economy in Sunshine Springs. And I'm sure you like it when the restaurant's busy, since you make more tip money that way. It must have been hard when the food poisoning thing happened. I hope you didn't miss out on too much income."

The waiter relaxed a little, and looked over at Theo. "Oh, you have no idea how awful that food poisoning incident was! Big Al was such a jerk! I was here the night he came in, and you could tell from the moment he walked through that door that he was spoiling for a fight. I'll tell you one thing: I know there's no way he got food poisoning from here. Bruce might be a bit of a character sometimes, but he takes pride in his food. He runs this place with military precision, and he doesn't like anything to be out of place or dirty. If there's even the slightest question whether food might not be perfectly fresh, he won't serve it."

Theo shook his head sympathetically, and I decided to keep my mouth shut and let him handle this. He was doing a much better job of getting information from the waiter than I had.

"It's really too bad that Bruce got tangled up with Big Al," Theo said. "He didn't deserve it, and I'm sure things have been difficult since the murder. I know the media is trying to pick on him. The nerve of those people, I tell you."

The waiter nodded enthusiastically. "Yes, the nerve! Exactly! Anyone who knows Bruce for more than two seconds knows that he would never hurt someone. He has too much integrity for that. Sure, he was angry about the food poisoning incident, but who wouldn't have been? That doesn't mean he would murder someone. In fact, he told us not to talk about it. He said the more that we talked about it, the more upset we'd get, and that that wasn't good for us. He said to let him take on the burden of dealing with Big Al and the media fallout. He really takes care of us and treats us well. Ask any of his staff here. They'll all tell you the same thing."

"I have no doubt they would," Theo said. "I'm just glad it seems to be blowing over. Speaking of staff though, I'd love to meet more of the staff here. The hostess seems so nice, and I'm sure all your fellow waiters are friendly and kind just like you. I need to make it out here more often. You're all doing a fine job."

Theo caught my eye across the table and smiled. I shook my head slightly in amazement. He had this waiter eating out of his hand already. I guess that was one benefit of being Theo Russo. You could go into any room and immediately people were falling all over themselves to make you happy. Now, our waiter seemed to have all but forgotten about me as he beamed at Theo.

"That means so much to me, Mr. Russo. I'll tell the staff what you said."

"You do that," Theo replied. "And, tell you what: I know you're all busy tonight, so no pressure…but tell your server friends to feel free to stop by and say hi."

The waiter promised he would, and hurriedly scampered off after he took our order, no doubt planning to tell everyone what Theo had said.

"I see what you did there," I said to Theo. "I should be rolling my eyes at how obviously you were buttering that waiter up, but it seems to have worked. So all I can say is thank you. Looks like we might get a chance to interview quite a few servers."

Theo winked at me. "Don't say I never did anything for you. Now, you want to tell me why Mitch asked you to investigate this murder? None of this makes sense to me."

CHAPTER TEN

"There is no big story, really," I said. "It's just that Mitch can't go anywhere without being chased down by the reporters. It doesn't help things that pictures of him in his wrestling costume made the national news. He feels like no one is taking him seriously, and that he can't make progress on this case because of that. He told me that since no one knows who I am, that I'm the perfect person to work on this."

Theo considered this for a moment. "I see. But isn't he worried that it's dangerous?"

I shrugged. "I guess not, since he put me on the case. He did offer to give me bodyguards and have his officers keep an eye on me." I paused, and then smiled. "And he gave me a bulletproof vest. I feel pretty official with that thing in my possession, although I haven't actually worn it out yet."

Theo gawked at me. "He gave you a bulletproof vest? It doesn't sound to me like he thinks there's no danger."

"The vest is just a precaution. This isn't as dangerous as the last murder case in Sunshine Springs."

Theo furrowed his brow. "Why not? Both cases involve murderers. Seems to me they're both pretty dangerous cases."

It looked to me like Theo was starting to grow a bit angry. He was drumming his fingers on the table faster and faster with each passing second, as though trying to contain anxious energy rising within him. I had a feeling that Mitch was going to get an earful about this later, and I searched for the words to try to calm the situation down a bit.

"Well, you know that the last case was extremely premeditated. I'm not sure this one was as meticulously planned. Sure, the criminal bought a monkey costume. But that didn't require as much planning as changing all the clues in a scavenger hunt like in the last case I worked on."

I hadn't let the danger stop me on any of the previous cases that I'd worked on, but I'd been trying to do better about heeding the advice of my friends. That's why I'd sworn off of sleuthing. But with Mitch's blessing, I was going to press forward on this case. I understood Theo's concern, but I also felt that if the town's sheriff was okay with things, then Theo was outvoted. Surely, Mitch knew better what was dangerous in a murder investigation than Theo did.

Theo must have realized from the look on my face that it would be useless to argue with me. He set his mouth in a hard line and shrugged. "Well, alright then. If that's what Mitch says…"

From the way he said it, I had a feeling that he was still going to be giving Mitch an earful about this later. I just hoped that Mitch wouldn't listen to him, and wouldn't tell me to get off the case. I mentally made plans to speed up my investigation as much as possible. There was no guarantee Mitch wouldn't change his mind at any moment and ask me to stop investigating. The sooner I could get this thing wrapped up, the better. Besides, there was a part of me that wanted to prove to Mitch that I could do this quickly. I wanted to show him that I was worthy of the trust he'd placed in me, and that I could outwit any murderer.

For now, I was saved from having to explain things further to Theo by the arrival of one of the other wait staff. A tall, redheaded girl with a generous splattering of freckles stopped by our table. She gave me a quick smile, but then directed all of her attention at Theo.

"Mr. Russo, Adam told me that he was waiting on you, and that you had been so kind and caring about the restaurant and asked how we were doing. I just wanted to stop by and say thank you." She paused, suddenly looking nervous. "I hope that's okay. He said that you wanted us to stop by. I hope he understood that correctly and I'm not bothering you…"

Theo smiled kindly at her. "Yes, I'm glad you stopped by. I know it's been a rollercoaster couple of weeks."

The girl looked relieved. "It has been! Things were so tough here after the alleged food poisoning incident. I wasn't making any money because we didn't have any business. I was starting to think that I would have to find a new job, which I really didn't want to do. Bruce is such a great employer. But, you know, I have bills to pay."

Theo nodded encouragingly. "Of course. I'm sure everyone understands that, especially Bruce."

The girl brightened. "But then, after the murder, things really picked back up. Not that I'm happy that Big Al died. No one here was a fan of him, but it was still quite a shock the way everything went down."

Theo nodded again. "It was a shock to everyone. We all understand."

The girl sighed. "It's been a crazy week in Sunshine Springs. But on the plus side, business has been booming here. I'm able to pay my bills again, as are the rest of the wait staff. I'm really happy for Bruce. He takes good care of us, and he didn't deserve to have his restaurant slandered the way Big Al did. I'm just glad that things are getting back to normal."

Then she lowered her voice slightly. "And I can't believe the way that the media is trying to portray him as a killer. Bruce wouldn't hurt a fly. He has a temper, sure. But it's all bark and no bite. I just hope the real murderer is found soon so that Bruce can get back to focusing completely on his restaurant."

Theo said a few more encouraging words to the girl, and then she took off to continue waiting on tables. Over the next several minutes, several more of the wait staff came by, all with a similar story: they'd been about to quit because they couldn't pay their bills, but Big Al's murder had miraculously revitalized the restaurant. Now, they could stay.

When Theo and I finally had a moment of quiet, I turned to him with a slight frown on my face. "You don't think it means anything that business has gone up at the restaurant since Big Al's murder, do you?"

Theo leaned back in his chair and swirled the wine in his wine glass. "You're asking if I think Bruce murdered Big Al to give his restaurant a boost?"

I nodded.

Theo shook his head. "No. It doesn't really make sense. How would he have known that a murder would somehow help the Spicy Grape? If you really think about it, it seems the other way around to me. I would have thought that a murder would have hurt rather than helped his restaurant. You'd think that when something bad happened to Big Al, the media would want to remind everyone of the other bad things that have happened to him: like the food poisoning incident. Which, of course, the media has been bringing up ad nauseam. But for some reason it's helping the Spicy Grape instead of hurting it."

"You're right," I admitted. But I must have sounded a little glum about it, because Theo laughed.

"Don't sound so forlorn," he said.

I sighed. "I know I shouldn't be sad to discover that Bruce isn't the murderer, but I was hoping to settle this case quickly. I want to prove to Mitch that I can do it."

Theo frowned at me, and his eyes darkened just a tad. "Trying to impress Mitch?"

I rolled my eyes at him and refused to answer. I wasn't in the mood to massage his ego and make him feel better about whether or not I was spending time with Mitch. I didn't understand why they had such a serious rivalry over me, anyway, since I had made it abundantly clear to both of them that I wasn't interested in dating.

The waiter arrived with our food at that moment, mercifully putting an end to that conversation. He set our food down, and I noticed a plate of something I didn't remember ordering. It looked a little bit like charred mushrooms.

Theo saw my confusion and grinned at me. "Truffles," he explained. "I whispered to the waiter to bring them when you were occupied with staring at the menu."

"Theo! These are extraordinarily expensive, and while I know that that might not be a big deal to you, I'm on a budget here. Sure, I'm expensing this to Mitch. But I don't think he'd be happy to see that I ate truffles on the police department's dime."

"Relax. It's my treat."

I scowled at him. "I don't want you to treat me. I don't want this to be a date! We're supposed to be splitting things evenly, but I can't afford even half a plate of truffles."

The more I ranted, the more amused Theo looked. He popped a truffle into his mouth and sat back with a grin.

"Izzy, you have to learn to lighten up. I know I'm always trying to find reasons to prove to myself that you're interested in me, but you have to understand that half the time I say those things it's because they rile you up. I might be hopeful, but I'm not an idiot. I know you don't want to date me right now. I'm just hoping to be around enough that when you are ready to date, I'll pop into your mind. But these? These are just truffles, not a marriage proposal. I have plenty enough money to pay for them in their entirety, and I'm not expecting you to go on a real date with me in return. Can you just enjoy the truffles as my friend?"

I relaxed a little and nodded, feeling sheepish. I realized then that I probably was acting a bit ridiculous by always being overly adamant about the fact that I wasn't interested in dating Theo. But I couldn't stop myself sometimes. I was a little gun-shy when it came to men, and I didn't want to lead Theo on and have him think I was being a tease.

I popped one of the truffles into my mouth, and my eyes widened. "These *are* really good."

Theo nodded. "Bruce won't give away who his supplier is, but everyone agrees that he has the best French truffles in wine country. I'm glad his restaurant is doing better, because I'd be really sad if I couldn't get these little guys anymore."

As I reached for another truffle, I saw movement out of the corner of my eye. My eyes widened as I saw that Bruce himself was heading toward our table with an angry scowl on his face. My heart started to pound, and I wondered if he knew that I was here to spy on him.

Was he going to chew me out in front of everyone? If he was innocent, then he probably wouldn't appreciate being investigated. But I had to be thorough in my detective work. Surely, he could see that, from an outsider's perspective, he was the likeliest suspect. I gulped down my truffle quickly, frantically trying to think of what I could say to appease him so that he didn't make a scene in the middle of the restaurant.

But when he approached the table, it wasn't me he spoke to. Instead, he stuck a finger right in Theo's chest. "You! I've got a bone to pick with you. Where have you been the last six months? I haven't seen you in here since even before that whole food poisoning debacle, and you know it makes me angry when my friends don't stop by."

I held my breath, not sure how Theo was going to respond.

Would he remain calm, or would he blow up right back at Bruce?

Theo calmly popped another truffle into his mouth and chewed it, raising an eyebrow in Bruce's direction. After he swallowed, he shrugged and said, "You can't blame me for not coming by. Why would I come see you when you smell so awful all the time? I know you can't help it that it's so hot back in that kitchen, and that it makes you constantly sweat. But seriously, dude. You ever hear of deodorant?"

My eyes widened, and I half-expected Bruce to start throwing punches at Theo. But then, Theo threw his head back and laughed, and Bruce did as well.

"Come here, you," Bruce said, and pulled Theo into a big bear hug. Both men started slapping each other on the back heartily, and I stared for several moments, still not entirely sure what was going on. Then, Theo turned and saw the look on my face. He laughed, and shook his head at me.

"It's alright, Izzy. He just likes to give me a hard time. He's right: I haven't been in for quite some time. But in my defense, I *have* been busy."

Bruce looked over at me, then back at Theo, and then winked. "You have been busy indeed."

When I realized what he was implying, I felt my cheeks go hot with embarrassment. "No! It's not like that. We're not dating we're just…" I wasn't sure what to say, when the real reason we were here was to investigate whether Bruce was a murderer. But as I stammered, trying to come up with some other explanation, Bruce started laughing again.

"Don't worry. I'm doing my best these days to stay far away from the gossip mill, so you don't have to worry that I'm going to say anything to anyone. I have to say, though, it's good to see you two so happy."

"It's not like that," I tried again. But Bruce wasn't really listening to me. He was slapping Theo on the back again, and saying he was happy that things were going so well for him. Theo thanked him—not bothering to explain that he wasn't actually dating me—and then asked him how he was holding up in light of Big Al's murder.

"Oh, you know," Bruce said as he waved his hand dismissively. "It's been a headache, but all I really care about is that my restaurant is doing well again."

I watched carefully as Bruce shook his head in amazement. I tried to see whether any guilt showed in his eyes, but as far as I could tell he appeared completely sincere.

I chewed my lower lip, feeling more frustrated than ever. This evening wasn't revealing any new information. All it was doing was making people think that Theo and I were a couple. I wasn't naïve. I knew that enough people had seen us here today that the gossip mill would probably be churning tomorrow. Of course, everyone would eventually realize that that wasn't correct, but it would be a headache in the meantime. And since I was no closer to solving this case after tonight, that headache would be all for nothing.

Okay, maybe not completely for nothing. I had at least determined that Bruce probably wasn't guilty. That would narrow down my search somewhat, making it likely that Tiffany or Jenny were the perpetrator.

Or maybe it was someone else entirely—someone whom I had no clues on yet. George's face flashed into my mind, and I remembered how he'd nearly mentioned to me the name of someone he thought was suspicious. Had he been intending to tell me he thought it was Bruce, or did he know something else about someone in Sunshine Springs? Was it possible he could give me a suspect I hadn't even thought of yet? I wasn't sure how easy it would be to get him to talk, but I definitely needed to try.

For the moment, I turned my attention back to Theo and Bruce, who were now discussing how delicious Bruce's truffles were.

"Come on," Theo was saying. "You can tell me where you get them. I won't tell anyone, I swear."

Bruce grinned and shook his head. "No way. You tell one person, and then all of a sudden everyone's ratcheting up the pressure to know. I'll take that secret to my grave with me."

Bruce laughed, and Theo grinned at him. "We'll see about that. I have ways of making people talk."

Before Bruce could come up with a reply, one of his wait staff was motioning frantically to him. "Uh-oh," he said. "Looks like someone needs my help. I better go. But don't you two worry. I'll make sure the staff takes good care of you."

He disappeared with a wink, and I gave Theo a death glare. "What was that all about? You're just going to let Bruce think we're on a date?"

Theo grinned at me. "Why not? I thought that's what you wanted people to think so that you had a good cover for why you were here at the fancy schmancy Spicy Grape."

"Well, not exactly. I just didn't want to raise any eyebrows, and I thought that coming here as Scott and Molly's third wheel when everyone knows they're dating would make people suspect that I was sleuthing again. But I thought maybe people would gloss over the fact that I was here if I was here with you."

I realized as soon as I said this how ridiculous it sounded. People didn't just gloss over Theo Russo. But I didn't take back my words. Instead, I filled my mouth with food so that Theo couldn't expect me to speak anymore.

He shook his head at me, still looking amused. "You're a funny one, Izzy."

I expected him to elaborate on that statement, but he didn't. Instead, he popped another truffle into his mouth, and then started in on the giant ribeye steak he'd ordered. I followed his lead and started eating my own food, but I felt unsettled and embarrassed.

Theo was right. Why had I thought coming here and acting like I was on a date would be a good idea? Theo couldn't go anywhere with a woman without people taking an interest, especially when that woman was me. Theo was the town's darling and the most eligible bachelor around, and it was no secret he'd taken an interest in me. But I'd gotten so caught up in the excitement of sleuthing that I hadn't been thinking clearly.

I vowed right then to change that. I would be more careful on how I approached things going forward.

At this point, I was ready for this fake date or whatever it was to be over. I ate quickly, and was already trying to come up with excuses for why I didn't want dessert when suddenly our waiter appeared again with a giant chocolate dessert and a bottle of champagne. I gave Theo another death glare, but he raised his hands in a gesture of surrender.

"Don't look at me. I didn't order this."

"Then why is it here?" I was irritated to the max now, and spoiling for a fight. Our waiter didn't seem to quite grasp the fact that there was a great deal of tension between us. Instead, he happily popped the champagne open and started pouring glasses.

"I know neither of you ordered this," he said cheerfully. "Bruce sent it over. He said to give many congratulations to the happy couple."

I groaned. So much for still trying to get out of here without everyone noticing that Theo and I were together—even though we weren't *actually* together. As the waiter spoke, I saw several couples across the room turning to look in our direction. Thankfully, most of them were tourists, so they wouldn't have much of an idea of what was going on. But there were a few Sunshine Springs locals, and I saw the glint in their eyes as they realized that they were witnessing prime gossip. By tomorrow, there were bound to be quite a few people talking about the fact that Theo Russo had finally snatched up Izzy James. I'd have to remember to text Molly later and tell her not to believe what she heard. If she thought that I was dating Theo without telling her, she'd be furious.

Bruce walked by just then and winked at us. "I don't have much time right now, because the kitchen is crazy busy. But I wanted to make sure you got my little gift. Are you all taken care of?"

"We're fantastic," Theo answered for both of us. I stared down at the chocolate cake and barely acknowledged Bruce. This had been a giant waste of time, and I couldn't wait to go home.

Unfortunately, it would be a while before I could go home. Now, there was a chocolate cake to eat and a bottle of champagne to drink—and Theo clearly wasn't interested in leaving until they were both done.

He remained in a good mood, chatting on and on about his winery and other town news. I only half-listened, because I was too busy thinking about the murder case. By the time we finished up the last of the champagne, the restaurant was clearing out. When the waiter brought the check, Theo tried to pay for it all, but I insisted on sharing the bill. I tried to make a big show of doing so, hoping that those around us would realize that this was just a friend thing and not really a date. But most of the couples left in the restaurant were from out of town, and the few Sunshine Springs locals that remained didn't seem to be paying much attention to us anymore. I supposed watching Theo with a girl got boring after a little while.

By the time we got out to the parking lot and Theo said goodbye to me, he seemed to have caught on to the fact that my mood had gone south. He reached over and gave my upper arm a friendly squeeze.

"Hey, don't be so grumpy. You got free champagne out of it, and everyone will realize soon enough that we're not actually dating. Unless, of course, you *want* to actually date. Then I'm happy to prove the rumors true."

I rolled my eyes at him, and said goodbye as quickly as I could. I rushed to my car and was speeding out of the parking lot before Theo even reached his car. I took a few deep breaths, and told myself to slow down. There was no sense in getting in a wreck just because I was annoyed with the way things had turned out.

I shouldn't have expected things to go any differently than they had. I had felt deep down that Bruce wasn't guilty, so I shouldn't have been surprised that I hadn't found any worrisome evidence against him by talking to his staff.

I also shouldn't have been surprised that being out with Theo would cause people to take notice. But Theo was right when he said that I shouldn't fret about it too much. Soon enough, people would realize that the rumors weren't true, and they'd be moving on to something else. I needed to focus on the murder investigation, and not on the gossip grapevine.

I started mulling things over in my head. If Bruce wasn't guilty, then who was? Tiffany and Jenny were the next suspects I needed to talk to, and I hoped that my efforts at interviewing them would bring me more information than a visit to Bruce's restaurant had brought.

I took a few breaths and slowly started to feel better. I couldn't expect to solve everything on the first night, and I would manage to win this case yet.

As I tried to give myself a pep talk, I was suddenly distracted by the sight of a bright yellow sports car up ahead. I squinted to see it better, and I would have bet money that the car belonged to Bruce, whom I knew owned a highlighter-yellow sports car. He must have been leaving the restaurant since things had slowed down, and I found myself suddenly feeling a bit guilty for having ever considered him a suspect. Of course, I knew that I had to investigate every angle. But I had to admit that even though I wanted to finish this case, I was glad he wasn't the guilty party. Hopefully Bruce could go home to his expensive house in his expensive neighborhood and relax. He deserved it.

But suddenly, I saw Bruce turn on a road that definitely didn't lead toward the upper class neighborhood I knew he lived in. In fact, I was pretty sure the road he was going down led nowhere but out of town. Frowning, I slowed down as I drove past the road. I saw his car bouncing away down the road, and then, on a sudden hunch, I killed my own headlights and spun onto the road to follow him. I had a gut feeling that the fact that he was going down this rather deserted road toward nowhere meant something.

I followed him for several minutes, wondering how far he was going to go, and trying to remember what the next town this road crossed would be.

I told myself I was just being paranoid. Bruce was probably just going to have dinner by himself somewhere other than a local restaurant. Goodness knows he couldn't go to any restaurant or bar in Sunshine Springs right now without being mobbed by media or spat on by the tourists who thought he'd killed Big Al. If I wasn't mistaken, the winding road eventually made its way into Napa Valley. There would be plenty of bars and restaurants for Bruce to choose from there, and the media probably weren't watching Napa very closely, if at all.

I was about to turn around, feeling foolish for even following Bruce, when he suddenly swerved and turned to the right. Almost instantly, he disappeared into an inky black grove of trees.

My heart started beating faster. Was it possible that there was something more to learn about Bruce, after all? I slowed down as I passed the spot near where he had turned. Without my headlights, I could just barely make out a narrow dirt road. Frowning, I wondered if it was the smartest idea to follow him alone down a road like this. But I never seriously considered turning around and giving up. Far too much curiosity burned within me.

I kept my distance, and kept my eyes trained on the bouncing headlights far in front of me.

Bruce turned down another dirt road, this one with huge no trespassing signs at its entrance. I ignored the signs and followed him. He turned down another road, then another, and another. I tried to focus on how many turns he'd made and where, hoping I'd be able to get out of there again.

Luckily, a few moments later my journey came to an end when I saw him approach a driveway that was gated. He punched a code into a keypad by the gate, and the gate creaked opened. I was dying to follow him in, but I knew I had to wait a few moments for him to drive away from the gate or he'd see me and get suspicious.

Unfortunately, the gate closed too quickly behind him, and there was no way I was getting in. But I still wasn't ready to give up. I drove a little ways past the gate and parked my car in what I hoped was a secluded enough spot that no one would notice it if they drove by.

I left my car and started slinking back toward the gate on foot. I hoped I could find a way to get in. My heart pounded in my chest, and I wondered whether I should call Mitch to tell him where I was, just in case. But after a few moments' consideration, I decided against it. Bruce was alone, and as long as I didn't let him know I was there, I should be safe enough. I didn't want to waste time on a phone call with Mitch, who was probably going to tell me to sit tight until he could send an officer to check things out. I knew that if I waited that long, I might miss out on an opportunity to see what was going on here.

I swallowed back my fear and pressed forward, eager to see what Bruce was doing. I could hardly contain my excitement at the thought that tonight might not have been a waste. Bruce was hiding something. I was sure of it. With every passing moment, I was suspecting more and more that he wasn't as innocent as he'd led me to believe back at the restaurant. There was only one way to know for sure: I had to see what was on the other side of this gate.

"I'm going in," I whispered through gritted teeth as I approached what appeared to be Bruce's secret hideout.

CHAPTER ELEVEN

My hopes of sneaking in on foot faded more with every step I took toward the gate. The trees and brush out here were thick, so I couldn't see much. But what I *could* see was that there was a giant electric fence surrounding this property. Warning signs were posted every few feet, assuring me that I would be jolted from here to infinity if I dared try to make it past the fence.

As I continued to creep along, I couldn't find any gaps wide enough for me to slip through. I kept walking, keeping a careful eye out so that if any video cameras were around I would spot them. I didn't see any cameras except for one on the keypad in front of the gate. I wasn't going to go anywhere near that keypad. I had no hope of guessing whatever the access code was, and I wasn't interested in giving Bruce a mug shot of me. I didn't want him to know I'd found his secret lair.

I shivered, and it wasn't just because the October night was cool. The very air around me felt sinister. What was waiting beyond that fence? A monkey costume? A murder weapon?

I had a feeling that something in there was related to Big Al's murder, although there must have been more beyond that gate than just a monkey suit and murder weapon. What did Bruce have in there that he needed to keep so secret? And had Big Al discovered it?

I'd thought all along that the food poisoning incident wasn't truly a strong enough motivation for Bruce to kill Big Al, even though I supposed people were killed for lesser reasons every day. But if Bruce was hiding something else in here that Big Al had discovered, maybe

Bruce had needed to keep him silent.

My phone buzzed in my pocket, nearly causing me to shriek in surprise. I caught myself just in time, and reached down to turn the ringer from vibrate to silent. Thankfully, it had at least been on vibrate instead of having the ringer turned up. In the stillness out here, Bruce would surely have heard a ringtone.

I glanced down at the message I'd just received and saw that it was from Grams, asking if I was going to come by and get Sprinkles, or whether he could spend the night with her. With a sigh, I texted to tell her I'd come get him the next day after work. I would have liked to have had him with me at that very moment, but I'd had to leave him behind tonight for obvious reasons. As much as I thought he'd fit in just fine at the Spicy Grape, not everyone agreed with me that dogs should be allowed in fine dining establishments.

I continued to walk up and down the fence for about fifteen minutes, but as I'd feared, there were no openings. I decided at last to give up and head back to my car. I'd tell Mitch about this place and he could get a warrant to come search it. As much as I would have liked to rush in and find a murder weapon that I could point Mitch directly to, I wasn't willing to risk being electrocuted by this fence in order to be the one who actually found the murder weapon.

Surely, since I'd found this place Mitch would still give me credit for solving the case—assuming, of course, that Bruce was indeed the guilty party. Until I knew for sure what he was hiding behind that electric fence, I couldn't be one hundred percent sure that he was guilty.

I had just started creeping back to my car when all of a sudden I saw headlights approaching from behind the gate. A few moments later, the gate slowly creaked open and I saw that Bruce was leaving whatever strange little complex this was. I flattened myself against a tree, unmoving. I wasn't too terribly far from the gate, and I worried that if he glanced in my direction he might notice my shadowy figure. My heart felt like it was pounding in my throat as he slowly passed through the open gate. If he saw me, I was done for.

Luckily, he didn't hang around long. He paused after clearing the gate, likely to make sure it was going to close behind him. As soon as it started closing, he peeled off onto the dark road as though he were taking off on a racetrack. Thankfully, he was heading back in the direction of town, so I knew he wouldn't see my car that I'd left parked in the opposite direction.

As I watched Bruce's rapidly fading taillights, I breathed a sigh of relief knowing that he wasn't going to catch me. The gate creaked as it slowly continued closing, and that's when it suddenly hit me that if I ran very, very fast, I might be able to get in before it shut completely.

I'd never been much of a sprinter, but I was pretty sure I set a personal record just then. I made a mad dash for the gate, feeling frantic as I watched the open portion of it shrinking. It was going to be close as to whether I could make it in time to squeeze through to the other side. I had a feeling I was going to end up running smack into the gate as it closed right before I got there, but I wasn't giving up now. I would do my best, and hope that the gate itself wasn't electric so that I didn't get electrocuted when I collided with it.

I squeezed my eyes shut as I neared the gate, which probably wasn't the smartest idea since I was running so fast. But I had no desire to actually see the moment that I collided with the big metal bars.

A few moments later, I suddenly found myself stumbling forward onto a gravel driveway. Confused, I opened my eyes and realized that I'd made it.

The gate was behind me! I hadn't collided with it, and I now stood on the inside. Adrenaline coursed through my veins, and I stared in disbelief. I had managed to get into Bruce's secret hideout!

It was then that I realized that I wasn't sure I'd be able to get back out. Just because Bruce had come out in his car didn't mean I would be able to get out on foot. Maybe there was a sensor that needed the weight of a car to open. Or maybe you needed a code just to get out.

Frantically, I looked around, hoping that I'd see something that would prove to be an easier way to get out than having to call Mitch to come rescue me. I saw a giant red button and walked hopefully over to it. The button said "Exit" on it in bright white letters, which I hoped meant that if I pushed it, the button would let me out.

I wasn't going to push it yet, though. I didn't know if it would alert Bruce, or sound some sort of alarm when pushed. I wanted to at least take a look around before I risked getting caught.

I crept down the gravel road, moving painfully slowly at first. I was terrified that at any moment I was going to set off a blaring alarm. But the further I went without incident, the more confident I became. I picked up my pace and grew less and less afraid of being caught and more and more excited about what I might find.

When the gravel pathway finally came out of the forest and into a clearing, I saw a large river meandering past a large building that stood only a few yards back from the river itself. The building was surrounded by another fence that warned of being electric. Bright red danger signs were posted every few feet, and although I walked the whole perimeter of the fence, I didn't see any way in. In addition to being electric, the fence was tall and had barbed wire at the top. Clearly, Bruce didn't want anyone to know what was in that building.

Dejectedly, I took a step back and tried to peer through the fence, being careful not to touch it and fry myself. Whatever was in the building wasn't visible from here, though. Everything was pitch dark, and all I could see inside were strange shapes that almost looked like trees. But I was sure that wasn't right. Why would Bruce have trees *inside* his secret building?

I had no idea what I was actually looking at, but I took several pictures on my cell phone, although I wasn't sure how well they would turn out. My cell phone was older and didn't exactly have a state-of-the-art camera, especially in light that low. I tried one photo with the flash on, but all I got was a bright view of the electric fence—and a horrible fright at how obvious the flash was in the dark of the clearing. I didn't think anyone was out there, but I didn't want to needlessly draw attention to myself.

After making a few more rounds around the building just to be sure that there was no other way in, I gave up on the building. I walked around the clearing a bit to see if I might find anything else of interest, but the building seemed to be the only exciting discovery I was going to make here. Finally, I started heading back toward the front gate. I told myself not to be disappointed that I hadn't gotten into the building. After all, I'd at least gotten into the front gate. That had to count for something.

It was late tonight, but in the morning I'd let Mitch know what I'd found here. Maybe he could get a search warrant, but there was nothing more I could do tonight. I crept back to the front gate and held my breath as I hit the exit button. I still half-expected an alarm to go off, as though the gate would know that I was an intruder and shouldn't be pushing any buttons here.

But no alarm went off. Instead, the gate slowly creaked open again. I took one last look behind me, knowing that if I left now I wouldn't be able to get back in. Had I really seen everything I wanted to? I considered for a moment, then nodded. I was sure there was nothing else here that I'd be able to get into tonight. And really, that was okay.

I'd seen enough to know that Bruce Burnham was not as innocent as he was leading everyone to believe.

CHAPTER TWELVE

The next morning, I headed to my pie shop early to bake pies. It was too early to actually call Mitch, so I sent him a text telling him to contact me as soon as he could. I had no doubt that as soon as he saw my message he would be contacting me immediately. He wanted this case solved just as badly as I did.

But as the early morning turned into the not-so-early-morning and I opened the café, I still hadn't heard from Mitch. I felt annoyed by this at first, but eventually I got so busy that I forgot to even think about it. Unfortunately, Mitch hadn't had an officer available to help me serve pie today, so I was once again by myself from open to close at the Drunken Pie Café. On the one hand, this annoyed me because it prevented me from sleuthing, and also prevented me from having a chance to talk to Theo or Molly about what I'd found the night before. But on the other hand, it wasn't so bad to be so busy. The nonstop pace at the café kept me from worrying too much about Bruce and his secret hideout.

In fact, the day flew by before I realized it. As I hung the closed sign on the front door of the café, I realized that I still hadn't heard from Mitch. I checked my phone again, and had no messages.

That was strange.

I felt a little tingle of worry starting to poke at my brain. It wasn't like Mitch to not contact me back, especially since he had given me this assignment and was waiting to hear from me. With a frown, I texted him again.

Hey, still waiting to hear from you. I hope you're alright?

It was a bit of ridiculous text. If he wasn't alright, my text wasn't going to do much to help. Still, I felt better at least letting him know I was thinking about him.

When I'd finished up all my closing duties, I still hadn't heard from him, so I decided to call the station and see if I could catch anyone there. Maybe I was being paranoid, but I just wanted to make sure that Mitch hadn't been kidnapped by a murderer or, perhaps worse, kidnapped by the crazy media that had been in our little town all week.

But the phone at the police station just rang and rang. I shouldn't have been surprised, since it was after six p.m. Unless somebody was working late, there was no reason for anyone to answer. Still, I had hoped. Now, I drummed my fingers on my sparkling clean café counter and wondered what to do. Finally, I pulled out my phone again, this time to text Theo.

Hey, have you heard from Mitch? I've been trying to get a hold of him all day and haven't heard back.

I stopped just short of saying that I was worried. I figured that was implied by the text, but I didn't want to sound too alarmist.

Theo texted back almost immediately.

Hey! I was just meaning to text you and see if you wanted to come by the winery to hang out. I feel a little badly about making fun of you last night. It's just that I really don't care if people think we're together. People can gossip if they want, but our relationship isn't any of their business. The important thing to me is that I like hanging out with you, as friends or otherwise. So, all that to say, do you want to come by? And to answer your question, no, I haven't heard from Mitch. I haven't tried talking to him today, though. I've been busy, and I figured he was too. Why? Something wrong?

Amused, I shook my head at the text as I scanned it.

"Way to write a novel in reply," I said with a smile. When Theo felt badly about something he could get awfully wordy, so I knew he truly felt badly about the way things had gone the night before. But it wasn't really his fault. I should have known things would get a bit awkward between us at the restaurant. I wasn't the least bit mad at him.

Still, I didn't want to hang out with him tonight. Not because I didn't want to see him, but because I wanted to continue my sleuthing efforts.

I chewed my lower lip for a moment, considering whether I

wanted to tell Theo about what I'd found the night before. Eventually, I decided against it. He would want to know every little detail, and I thought it was probably best if I told Mitch first. If the way Theo had acted last night was any indication, he was good friends with Bruce. I was worried he might get upset if he thought Bruce was hiding some big secret, and then go confront Bruce in a fit of anger. That was the last thing I needed right now. I didn't want Mitch to lose the element of surprise when he went to check on Bruce's hideout.

So I texted Theo back a quick reply, declining his invitation. *Hey, don't worry about last night. I admittedly overreacted a bit. Unfortunately, I'll have to take a rain check on the chance to come to the tasting room. You know I love your pinot, but I have a lot to do tonight. Maybe on the weekend?*

Theo texted me back a frownie face, then another text that said, *Okay, fine. If you really are too busy for me. But I'm holding you to this weekend.*

I shrugged, and slipped my phone into my purse. Maybe by this weekend I would have solved the Big Al murder case, and I could relax a bit and sip wine with Theo.

Or maybe, I'd be just as confused as I was now, and wouldn't want to spend any time away from the trail of clues.

Those were worries for another day. Right now, I wished that I would hear from Mitch. But since the sheriff still wasn't calling me back, I decided the best thing to do was to continue with my investigation. Yes, I was pretty sure at this point that Bruce was the guilty one. Why else would he have a hideout if he wasn't doing something shady like murdering people? But it was probably still good to cover all my bases and interview Jenny and Tiffany. I knew from the case file that Jenny lived in a small apartment not too far from the Drunken Pie Café, so I decided I would run down there to see if she would talk to me. I'd have to come up with some reasonable excuse for talking to her that didn't involve "I'm investigating you for murder," but I'd think of something.

Before I left, I briefly considered whether I should put my bulletproof vest on, but I decided against it. It was bulky and rather obvious even underneath my baggy hoodie, and I felt like Jenny would think I was a weirdo for wearing one. Besides, I didn't think Jenny was dangerous. I doubted she was the murderer, and talking to her couldn't be any more dangerous than sneaking into Bruce's hideout last night had been.

I did sort of wish I had Sprinkles with me to stay by my side and guard me, but he was still with Grams. I didn't want to burn time going to pick him up and then driving back here to talk to Jenny, so I decided I'd just have to trust that I'd be okay without my trusty dog around to help save me if anything went wrong.

Through the front window of my café, I could still see the news media. Several reporters paced slowly up and down Main Street, still trying to snag unsuspecting passersby and get something interesting from them to keep the story of Big Al's murder investigation going. I knew the news crews were getting desperate. Several days had passed without any new information, and the journalists needed to come up with something else to say to keep people on the edge of their seat.

That wasn't my problem, though, and I wasn't interested in helping them keep their viewership. I was interested in avoiding them, which is why I decided to walk down the back alley to Jenny's house. Staying off Main Street would keep me from having to deal with any obnoxious journalists on the short trek. I hurried along, thankful for the chance to breathe some fresh air even though my legs were tired from standing all day.

I had nearly reached the back of the building where Jenny's apartment was located when I suddenly felt two hands grab me firmly and pull me back into a smaller side alley that extended from the main back alley. I started to shriek, but one of my captor's hands quickly moved to cover my mouth firmly. But this meant that even though I couldn't shriek, my attacker was only holding me with one hand, making it easier for me to potentially wriggle away.

I wished more than anything then that I had worn my bulletproof vest and had kept Sprinkles with me for the day, even though I knew he would have been bored to death in the back of the café. He would have come in quite useful in that moment—he might not look like a typical guard dog, but he protected me fiercely.

He wasn't here right now, though, so I'd have to defend myself. I began flailing about in an attempt to escape, but stopped when I heard a voice that sounded oddly familiar.

"Stop! Calm down! I'm not going to hurt you. I just need to talk to you."

With that, the hand that was still gripping me released me.

I spun around, my own hands balled into fists and ready to fight, but that's when I realized that Jenny was standing in front of me. I didn't know her that well, but her voice had sounded familiar because the few times that I had turned on the news in the last few days, I'd inevitably heard her being interviewed.

"Jenny? What's going on?"

She stood taller and looked me square in the eyes. "I need your help."

"My help?"

I was confused. I'd never really spoken with Jenny before, and as far as I knew she didn't know me from Adam. But she was nodding at me, looking quite certain.

"Yes, your help. I know you're helping Mitch with Big Al's murder case."

I tried to play dumb. "What are you talking about? I'm a pie shop owner, not a detective."

Jenny put a hand on her hip. "I've been watching the police station quite a bit, trying to see from afar whether anyone was coming or going that might have given me an indication that this murder was actually being solved. So far, it doesn't seem that any progress has been made, but I saw you go in and talk to Mitch. You were in there way too long to have just been delivering pies like you told the media. He asked you to help on the case, didn't he?"

I paused for a moment, trying to figure out how to answer her. There was no way I was actually going to tell her that Mitch had asked me to take over the case. But she was right. I had definitely been there too long for a mere pie delivery—a fact that had escaped the news media. Maybe the news crews figured that I was catching up on the latest gossip on the case, but Jenny would have known better. She knew that Mitch never gave up anything on his cases that easily, not even to his closest friends. Theo was the only one Mitch confided in on a regular basis.

Jenny gave me a long, hard look. "Don't try to deny it. Your hesitation tells me all I need to know. I know you and Mitch are friends, I know you helped on cases in the past, and I know he would need your help on this case with all the crazy media constantly stalking him."

I still didn't answer. There was no use denying that I had worked on cases in the past. True, it hadn't been with Mitch's blessing. But everyone in Sunshine Springs knew that I had helped to catch a murderer or two.

But then, I realized that denying that I was helping on the case wasn't the smartest move, anyway. If I played along with Jenny, this might be just the opening I needed to be able to talk to her. She was practically begging me for my help, after all. Maybe a golden opportunity had just landed in my lap.

Why she was begging me for help, though? Did the fact that she needed my help mean that she was innocent and wanted me to help prove it? Or was she starting to feel the heat of the investigation, and did she think that I could help her draw attention away from herself? Of course, she would probably never actually put it that way, but maybe she thought she could frame someone else and convince me that they committed the murder when it had really been her.

I had no idea what was actually going on here, but I was interested to hear what she had to say.

"I'd like to help you, Jenny," I said, trying to sound sympathetic. "But what could I possibly do for you that Mitch couldn't?"

Jenny looked around before answering, as though worried someone had snuck into the alley and was listening to us. A brisk breeze was picking up, and she shivered. She wasn't wearing a jacket even though the October air was chilly, and her t-shirt only had short sleeves. She seemed like she was a bit of a mess at the moment, and I tried to decide whether this was a sign of guilt or innocence. Honestly, after what I'd seen at Bruce's hideout last night, I was inclined to think Jenny was innocent. But, like I'd told myself earlier, I needed to cover all my bases. I forced myself to patiently wait for her to answer me.

Finally, she lowered her voice and spoke. "I know who killed Big Al, and I need your help proving it."

I felt my heart beating faster with excitement—although I forced myself to remember that just because she said she knew who the killer was didn't mean she actually did. If she needed help proving it, then she must not have any actual proof. Was she just trying to blame someone else to get herself off the hook?

All these thoughts went through my head in rapid succession, but all I said was, "Okay...?"

Jenny looked right and left again, then leaned in and whispered in my ear. "It was Tiffany."

I resisted the urge to roll my eyes. "You'll have to forgive me if

I'm a bit skeptical. Everyone knows you two were fighting, so of course you're going to blame her."

Jenny winced. "I know it probably seems that way, but I promise that I'm not just trying to spite Tiffany without anything to back up my words. I can tell you more, but not out here. Will you come to my apartment with me? I can explain more there, and I have something to show you."

I hesitated for just a moment, weighing the wisdom of going back to the apartment of a potential murderer—especially a potential murderer who had figured out that I was working on the case. Was she just trying to get rid of me so that I wouldn't be able to find evidence on her?

Now I really wanted that bulletproof vest. Or Sprinkles. Or both.

But the more I thought about it, the more it seemed to me that if Jenny wanted to take me out, there were probably better ways to do that than invite me back to her apartment, especially after revealing that she did indeed know that I was working on the case. Why would she show all her cards and lose the element of surprise if she just wanted to eliminate me?

Feeling a little bit better about following her, I nodded. "Okay, I'll go with you. But let's make it quick, and this better not be a waste of my time."

Jenny's eyes lit up, and she reached over to squeeze my hand as though we were best friends. "It's not a waste of time, I promise. I think this will really help you in your investigation."

I tried not to grimace at her touch. I reminded myself that just because she was an alleged murderer didn't mean I should treat her like a social outcast. Innocent until proven guilty, right?

With a nod, I followed her as she began walking down the alley toward her place. I should be excited about this. I'd been looking for an excuse to talk to her anyway, and here she was begging me to discuss the case. Not only that, but she was promising me information that would prove to me who the killer was. I couldn't have asked for things to go more smoothly.

So why couldn't I shake the feeling that something wasn't right about this?

CHAPTER THIRTEEN

I don't know what I expected Jenny's apartment to look like. She always appeared to be such a mess when speaking to the media, or when she was out in public fighting with Tiffany. I had expected the inside of her apartment to be just as chaotic as her public persona.

But nothing could have been further from the truth. Jenny had furnished the apartment with a few tasteful, sleek pieces: a table and chairs, a couch, and some bookshelves with a modern look.

She also kept the place spotless. Either that, or she had cleaned incessantly in preparation for my arrival.

"Do you want something to drink?" Jenny asked. "I have sparkling water, a few cans of soda, or I could make some coffee."

She sounded nervous, and when I looked at her I saw that she was wringing her fingers slightly. Either she truly had something really big to tell me, or she was lying and was afraid I was going to find out. But even though I'd never spent that much time with her, the more time I did spend with her, the more she seemed fairly genuine to me. Either she was being truthful, or she was a really good actress. I just found it strange that her flashy public persona didn't match this private, dialed-down version of herself. But there was only one way to figure out if she was telling me the truth when she said she had information on the killer, and that was to hear her out on what she actually had to say.

I decided to decline the offer of a drink, determined instead to get information from her as quickly as possible. "No, I'm alright. Goodness knows I've already had enough coffee at the café today anyway, and I'm not really thirsty. Why don't you just tell me what it was you couldn't say out in the middle of the street?"

Jenny nodded, but did pour herself a large glass of water, guzzling it down before speaking again. "I have something to show you."

She grabbed a key from a drawer in her kitchen and disappeared down a hallway that I assumed led to her bedroom. When she returned, she held a small stack of letters, which she placed on the counter in front of me.

"These are letters Tiffany mailed to me. You can see the addresses on the envelope, along with the postmarks. They were all sent to me through the Sunshine Springs post office in the days before Big Al was murdered. I know that's Tiffany's handwriting, because I've personally seen her writing things out before. Of course, the police won't want to take my word for it. They'll have to get handwriting experts, or whatever it is they do to verify these things. But I promise you: this is definitely Tiffany's writing."

I gingerly picked up one of the letters, looking at the postmark just as Jenny had suggested. And just as she'd said, it was postmarked from Sunshine Springs a few days before Big Al's murder. The addresses did indeed list Tiffany as the sender and Jenny as the recipient. True, anyone could have put anyone's name and address on the envelope and dropped the letter into the mail. But I didn't see any reason for Jenny to lie about the fact that she recognized the handwriting as Tiffany's. It wouldn't make sense to try to fool me about something that could be so easily verified.

"Go on. Open it," Jenny said a bit impatiently. My heart pounded with excitement as I opened the envelope. The letter was written in the same large, flowery script as the address on the outside had been. It looked as though it had been written in a hurry, and it was punctuated with an excess of exclamation points, giving it a bit of an angry look.

I scanned the words quickly, finding a long tirade against Jenny that accused her of trying to steal Big Al from Tiffany. That wasn't unexpected, and I was beginning to think that I was indeed wasting my time being here with Jenny—until I made it to the last line.

I'm warning you, leave Big Al alone. If I can't have him, then I'm going to make sure no one can.

I stared at the words in shock, rereading them several times. This sounded like much more than just a simple catfight over a man. It sounded suspiciously as though Tiffany was making an actual threat on Big Al's life. Had she really gone that crazy, that she would have killed him just so Jenny couldn't take him away from her?

I read through several more of the letters without saying a single word to Jenny. From the hopeful look on her face, I could see that she knew that she had at least interested me.

The rest of the letters were similar. They were long rants about how Big Al loved Tiffany more than Jenny, and that Jenny was a horrible human being for trying to steal him from her. But the rants weren't the disturbing parts. The disturbing parts were at the end, where inevitably Tiffany would make a threat very similar to the one that I had read in the first letter.

There were six letters: one had been sent every day in the six days leading up to Big Al's murder. Unsurprisingly, there were no letters postmarked after the date of the murder.

When I finally finished going through all of them, I sat back and looked up at Jenny with wide eyes. Jenny looked visibly relieved when she saw the expression on my face.

"See? I told you I have proof. That really makes it look like Tiffany is the killer, doesn't it?"

"It does," I admitted. "But why in the world have you been holding onto these? I know that you had to give a statement to the police, and I know they searched your apartment. If you knew you had these, why not mention it to the police, or why not show them the letters when they came to go through your apartment?"

Jenny fidgeted, then looked up at me with a proud smile on her face. "I don't want the police to know where my secret hiding place is. They didn't let me come home before searching the apartment, so if I had given them the papers then, they would have known where my hiding place was."

I stared at her, thinking that this must be a joke. "You've been holding on to evidence in a murder case because you don't want the police to find a secret hiding place? Even if you didn't want to give the letters to them when they first came to search your place, surely at some point in the last week you could have found the time to take the letters down to the station?"

Jenny frowned at me. "And what? Tell them they missed them when they were here? They're going to want to know where they came from. I can't let the police know the letters are from me, or I'm going to have to show them my secret hiding place. Nobody is allowed to see my secret hiding place. It's special."

I frowned at her. "I'm sure if you explained this to Mitch that he could make sure that it was kept secret, and that only those who absolutely needed to would see it."

But Jenny shook her head, apparently determined to not let anyone know about her secret little spot. I wanted to roll my eyes at her, but I didn't think that would be a helpful way of convincing her to give up more information about this. Instead, I tried to reason with her a bit more.

"Come on, Jenny. You want Big Al to receive justice, don't you? For evidence of his murder to be taken seriously, the police need to know where it actually came from. I promise: Mitch is very good at keeping secrets. He knows all sorts of secrets about numerous Sunshine Springs citizens, and he's never breathed a word of them to me or anyone else. He won't reveal any more information than is absolutely necessary, and he definitely won't tell the press that he got the letters from you. So if that's what you're worried about, you can relax. Mitch hates the way the news media have taken over the town."

But Jenny was still shaking her head. "No way. I don't care how much you say Mitch won't reveal secrets. I don't want anyone to know my secret hiding place, not even him."

I frowned as I looked at Jenny's stubborn expression, and I couldn't help thinking about Bruce and his strange, gated hideout. What was it with everyone and their secret hiding places? What could Jenny possibly have to hide that would make her so adamant about not showing anyone her hiding place? Was there something more that she wasn't sharing that might implicate her in the murder as well? Were these letters from Tiffany just a distraction to keep her from looking guilty?

My frown deepened as I had this thought, but then I thought about Bruce again. If Jenny was the guilty one, then what was Bruce hiding?

Then, I had an even crazier thought. Was it possible that Jenny's hiding place was the same as Bruce's, and they were working together?

The possibilities were going to drive me crazy, but at the end of the day what I really wanted was for Jenny to let me take these letters to Mitch. If that meant I had to play along for the moment and act like I actually cared about her hiding place, then so be it.

"I really think you should tell Mitch everything, but if you want I can tell him that I have evidence but that he has to promise not to ask about the location. He won't be happy about that, but I think I could convince him to agree that he won't make you show him the exact hiding place they came from."

I thought that would be good enough for Jenny, but she was shaking her head. "No, I don't just want him to promise not to ask me where it came from. I don't want him to know that this came from me at all."

I stared at her, trying to understand. "But Jenny, the letters are addressed to you. Who else would they have come from?"

Jenny waved her hand as though this was no big deal. "Tell him that an anonymous source gave them to you. You can say that the source intercepted them before they were delivered to me, that way Mitch doesn't have to know that I'm the one who gave them to you, and he won't come asking me about my hiding place."

I raised an eyebrow at Jenny, starting to think that she really was a big ditz after all. There was no way I could convince Mitch that I got these papers from an anonymous source. He was going to figure out in about two seconds that Jenny had been the one to give them to me. Besides, for evidence to be admissible in court, there had to be a chain of custody established, and I could see the chain of custody rapidly breaking down here. You couldn't exactly throw some letters in front of a judge or jury and say "They came from an anonymous source, but don't worry! They're totally real!"

With this in mind, I decided to try one more time to explain things to Jenny. "If I show this to Mitch, even if I don't tell him I got it from you, he's going to figure it out. Besides, it's better for the case against Tiffany if we know exactly where it came from."

But Jenny wasn't budging on the issue. She shook her head adamantly. "Either you agree to tell Mitch these letters came from an anonymous source, or I'm taking them back and you won't have any proof they ever existed. Trust me, you'll never find my hiding spot, and if you try to sic Mitch and his officers on me, I'll deny everything. He'll think you're crazy for suggesting that I ever had these letters. So that's my offer. Take it or leave it. Either you present the letters as from an anonymous source, or they disappear and you're back to square one on solving this murder case."

It wasn't exactly true that I'd be back to square one. Jenny could take away the letters, but she couldn't take away the fact that I now knew that Tiffany was a strong suspect in the case. I may not have the letters anymore, but I could go interrogate Tiffany and perhaps find something else to prove her guilt.

But why make this harder on myself than it had to be? Jenny was acting ridiculous, but if promising to tell Mitch this was from anonymous source was what she wanted, then I would promise that. As long as I didn't actually tell Mitch myself that I got the letters from Jenny, she couldn't be mad at me. I'd tried to warn her that Mitch would know it was her. It wasn't my fault if she didn't want to listen.

"Okay. I won't tell Mitch it was you. Do you have a Ziploc bag or something I can put these in? I've already been contaminating this evidence enough by getting my fingerprints on it, although I think the handwriting analysis is going to be what makes these letters valid."

Jenny beamed at me, then went to get me a bag. "I knew you could help me! I just knew it! Everyone says you're the best amateur sleuth around, and it's true. Thank you so much!"

I didn't feel like I'd done anything particularly amazing today. Jenny had dropped this clue in my lap, so I couldn't exactly take credit for my amazing sleuthing skills. But still, as I left her house with the bag of new evidence, I couldn't keep myself from imagining how proud Mitch was going to be at the progress I'd made. The letters would give him a new reason to interrogate Tiffany, and I still thought that there might be something worth finding at Bruce's secret lair. Perhaps all of this was connected somehow. Was it possible that there had been a conspiracy, and that some of the main suspects had been working together to get Big Al?

There were still a lot of pieces that needed to be put together, but I was making progress.

I practically skipped back to my café, where my car was still parked. I needed to pick up Sprinkles, and then hopefully I'd have a chance to talk to Mitch. Maybe I could even schedule a time to talk to Mitch in person tonight.

But when I got into my car and pulled out my phone to check for messages, I still didn't have anything from Mitch. I frowned, trying not to worry.

You okay? I texted him, even though I didn't expect an answer at this point. Still, I had to try.

As I drove towards Grams' house to get Sprinkles, I couldn't completely squelch my worries. Maybe this case was turning out to be more dangerous than Mitch had initially thought, and maybe Mitch had somehow gotten himself tangled up in that danger. I shivered, and tried to push the thought from my mind. There must be a reasonable explanation for Mitch's silence.

There must be a reasonable explanation for *everything* in this case. At least, I hoped so. And I hoped I would find the murderer before anyone else got caught up in this mess.

CHAPTER FOURTEEN

After picking up Sprinkles, I decided to take him for a walk. I felt badly that I hadn't spent much time with him in the last few days, and besides, I needed to clear my head and a walk seemed like a good way to do that. I still hadn't heard from Mitch, and I wasn't sure I wanted to move forward with anything else until talking to him. I knew I needed to talk to Tiffany, but before I did I wanted to see what Mitch thought about Tiffany's letters and Bruce's hideout.

But Mitch had gone completely silent. I tried calling him again, and even tried calling the police station although I knew it wasn't likely that anyone would be there at this time of night. I consoled myself with the knowledge that if something was wrong I would surely have heard about it by now. None of today's gossip had been about anything bad happening to Mitch, so he must have just been extraordinarily busy.

Still, it was so strange for him not to contact me back, and I couldn't help but fret. I didn't want to look like some desperately crazy worrywart, though, so I continued walking calmly with Sprinkles. I told myself that I just needed to give him time to answer me.

In the meantime, I tried to sort through the thoughts in my head. Something didn't feel right about what Jenny was saying, but I couldn't put my finger on it. Her story about the secret hiding place seemed bizarre. If she was hiding something big in her hiding place, why didn't she just move it before showing the cops her secret hiding place? It all seemed a little too fabricated if you asked me.

My next step was definitely talking to Tiffany, but for the moment I felt stuck. I felt like I was getting a hazy picture of what had happened, but the haze was still too great to pinpoint any one person.

That's when I remembered that there was someone in town who perhaps could pinpoint one single person for me: George Drake. I hadn't talked to him since the night I dropped him off after the murder, and I wondered whether he might be more willing to talk now that he'd had a few days to process everything.

Feeling energized again, I walked back to my car and started driving toward George's house. Sprinkles sat in the passenger seat, pushing his wet nose against the window and making smeary nose marks no matter how many times I asked him to stop.

I didn't have the heart to reprimand him too sharply. He seemed so excited to be on an adventure with me, and I reached over to scratch him behind his ears.

"Having fun, boy? I'm glad you're here with me. I know Grams likes seeing you, and I know you like spending time with her. But it's been too quiet at the shop without you around. Maybe once this whole mess settles down we can take a day off and go do something fun just the two of us. It would help if I found an employee for the café, but even if I don't, we can close the pie shop for one day. Tourist season is ending, and I'm sure the Sunshine Springs residents will understand."

Sprinkles woofed excitedly in response, and moved his nose away from the window just long enough to give me a big, sloppy kiss on my cheek. I laughed, feeling like everything was right in the world despite the uncertainty that still hung over the town because of Big Al's murder.

When I reached George's house, I was happy to see that light streamed out into the front yard from many of his windows. I'd been worried he might not be home. If I were him, I probably would have gotten out of Sunshine Springs for a week or two to avoid the press of media. But perhaps George stayed because he had such a strong interest in seeing how the investigation of his good friend was going.

I walked up the long path to his door with a new spring in my step. I had a feeling that talking to him would make me feel better, even if I couldn't convince him to give me the information he knew. He would at least be glad to hear me discuss all of my clues, and maybe discussing them out loud with someone else would help me make some sense of all of this.

Sprinkles was tagging along beside me, his tail wagging wildly. I wasn't sure whether George was a dog person, or whether he would allow Sprinkles inside, but I figured it couldn't hurt to ask. That was assuming George was going to invite *me* in, of course. I couldn't be sure of that, either. But he had seemed excited enough to have company the last time I was here. Hopefully he would feel the same way today.

As I approached the door and was about to ring the doorbell, my optimism quickly evaporated. I heard yelling on the other side of the door, and I paused with my finger inches from the doorbell to listen to the ruckus coming from inside. I couldn't make out the words, but George was definitely screaming at someone. After a few moments, he went silent and I didn't hear anything. Then, a few moments later, he was yelling again. He must have been on the phone with someone, but who? And why were they making him so upset?

For a moment, I considered leaving. Perhaps I had come at a bad time. But then, a small prick of worry kept me from turning around and heading back to my car. George sounded really upset. What if he needed help? Maybe there was something I could do for him. True, I didn't know him well. But I felt that we had at least forged a small friendship the night I drove him home. I didn't know how many friends he had in town in the wake of Big Al's murder, and maybe he just needed someone to be there for him right now. I should at least check on him.

Besides, if I left now, who knew when I would have a chance to come back and talk to him again? If he yelled at me and told me to leave, then so be it. I'd been yelled at plenty of times in my life. But maybe he would actually want to talk.

Taking a deep breath, I rang the doorbell before I could change my mind. George, who had been in the middle of yelling, suddenly stopped. I heard him walking toward the door, and he must have looked through the peephole to see that it was me. He started speaking into the phone again, but in a normal tone instead of a yelling one. Even though I couldn't actually make out the words he was saying, I got the feeling he must be telling the person on the other side of the line that he needed to go. A few moments later, there was a brief silence, which was then broken by the sound of the deadbolt being unlatched. Then, the door opened to reveal a sheepish-looking George standing in front of me.

"Oh goodness! How much of that did you hear! I'm so embarrassed."

I smiled kindly. "I didn't hear that much. I couldn't make out any of the words, but it sounded like you were a little upset. Are you okay?"

I tried to make my voice sound sympathetic. I didn't want him to think I was here to judge him.

He sighed, and motioned for me to come in. Then he suddenly noticed that there was a Dalmatian sitting next to me.

"Oh! This must be Sprinkles. I've heard so much about him! Everyone around town loves him." He bent down and held out a hand to Sprinkles. "Nice to meet you. I'm George."

Mercifully, Sprinkles remembered his manners and dutifully put a paw up to shake George's hand.

George beamed. "What a charming dog! Bring him in as well."

Sprinkles' tail wagged harder at this. He looked at me, and let out an excited yip, and I could have sworn I saw a smile turning up his doggy lips. I ruffled his ears, then followed George into the house.

"Whiskey?" George asked, then laughed as he turned to look at me. "Just kidding. I remember you don't like whiskey. What about a glass of white wine instead? It's an absolute certainty that anyone who doesn't like whiskey will like white wine, and anyone who doesn't like white wine will like whiskey. It's a universal law of drinking."

I laughed. "I'll take a glass of white wine. But just a small one. I still have a lot of stuff to do tonight."

"Coming right up." George walked over to the small bar in his living room and started pouring drinks: whiskey for himself and a glass of Chardonnay for me. As he handed me my glass, he shook his head and looked quite embarrassed.

"I can't believe you heard me yelling like that. I swear, I'm not usually such a short-tempered person. But Big Al's funeral arrangements aren't going well. As one of Big Al's friends, I was trying to help plan everything, but there are too many people trying to help. Everyone wants something different, and the funeral has turned into some big circus. I'm just not sure that's what Big Al would have wanted." George shook his head sadly. "He would have wanted to be laid to rest with dignity."

I chewed my lower lip, considering this. The Big Al I had seen around town seemed to love drama, so it seemed to me that he would have loved a funeral that amounted to a giant circus. But what did I really know? Maybe the larger-than-life Big Al had just been the public persona he projected, and with his close friends he was a more laid-back sort of person.

"I'm sorry things are so stressful," I said as I took a sip of my wine. It tasted heavenly, and I wondered how much this bottle had cost. It was definitely the best Chardonnay I'd ever tried in my life.

George let out a long sigh and took a sip of his whiskey. "I have to say that I'll be glad when this funeral business is all over. Maybe it seems like a strange thing to say, but I feel like I can't truly mourn Big Al until all the hullabaloo surrounding his death is done."

I nodded sympathetically. "That totally makes sense. When's the funeral?"

George let out a long, frustrated sigh. "Tomorrow. In Los Angeles. I wanted his funeral to be in San Francisco, since that's where he spent the last couple years of his life, and since he made no secret of his hatred for Los Angeles. But I lost that battle. There are too many celebrities who want the funeral to be in Los Angeles because they see this as some sort of big publicity event." He shook his head sadly. "I'm not a big fan of L.A. but for the sake of paying my respects to Big Al, I'll be flying there tomorrow. The sooner this is all over, the better."

"Los Angeles?" I repeated as I took another sip of my wine. "I wonder if Jenny or Tiffany are going. I just saw Jenny today, and she didn't mention anything about the funeral."

"They'd better not be going!" George exclaimed. "Those two gold-diggers were just trying to cash in on Big Al's fortune. Did you know that Jenny is in talks with a media company about a reality show based on finding love now that she's lost her once-in-a-lifetime celebrity crush?"

My eyes widened. "No, I didn't know. She conveniently forgot to mention that."

"Of course she did. She probably knows better than to talk about such nonsense with you. She knows you'd try to set her straight, just like I tried to set her straight when she made the mistake of telling me. But she didn't listen to me, and she wouldn't have listened to you. She's just trying to cash in on all of this as best she can."

George angrily sipped his whiskey, and I felt quite sorry for him. There was no mistaking that it had been a rough week for any true friend of Big Al. It might have been my imagination, but it seemed to me like George's face was a bit paler than the last time I'd seen him, and he looked like he'd lost a few pounds as well—which was a bit alarming considering it had only been a few days since I'd seen him. The stress of this was obviously getting to him.

"How are you holding up?" I asked, hoping he could hear the sincerity in my voice. I really did feel sorry for him right now.

He looked at me and shrugged, but he seemed grateful that I'd asked the question. "I'm doing my best to hang in there. It's not easy with the media here and the funeral arrangements going so crazy. I've mostly been hiding in my house and trying to stay out of the crossfire. Hopefully Mitch can get this case solved soon so that things can get back to normal." George paused and sniffed. "Well, at least as normal as they can be now that Big Al is gone."

Here, I saw my opening to talk to George about the murder investigation, but I found myself feeling quite nervous. Would he approve of the fact that Mitch had asked me to help? Or would he think that Mitch putting an amateur sleuth on the case was more proof of the incompetence of everyone surrounding Big Al's murder? I remembered that on the day of the murder he hadn't wanted to talk to the police at all. Was he still angry at the police? And would that anger extend to me if he knew I was working with the police?

There was only one way to find out. I took a deep breath and forced myself to speak before I could change my mind. "Actually, believe it or not, Mitch asked for my help on the investigation into Big Al's murder. He needed help from someone the media doesn't recognize, and, as you might have heard, I've done a bit of detective work on some other murder cases here in Sunshine Springs." I smiled widely, holding my breath and hoping that George wasn't going to start yelling at me.

George set his whiskey down and looked at me with wide eyes. "Really? Mitch put you on the case?"

His expression was unreadable, and I nervously nodded my head. "I promise that I'm going to give this my absolute best effort. I know I might not technically be a police officer, but I was a lawyer before moving to Sunshine Springs, so I do understand the way law enforcement works. And I really care about keeping the streets of

Sunshine Springs safe. And, of course, I care about finding your friend's killer. I hope you don't think it's presumptuous of me to get involved."

"Are you kidding me?" George asked.

It took me a moment to realize that the question was not rhetorical. He really did want to know if I was kidding him.

"Nope," I said, my heart dropping. This didn't seem to be going well, but I tried to keep my voice upbeat. "I'm really helping out."

There was a short pause, and then George started clapping his hands. "That's fantastic! Really, this is the best news I've heard all week. Finally, someone who knows what they're doing is on this case!"

I felt a rush of relief. For a moment, I'd thought that George was about to kick me out of his house, yelling and screaming at me about how the only thing more incompetent than the police was a civilian trying to help the police. But he seemed genuinely pleased about my involvement in the case.

"That's actually another reason I came by," I said. "Of course, I wanted to check on you and make sure you're doing okay. But I also wanted to see if you had any information you'd be willing to share with me about who you think might have committed the murder. I know you said when I dropped you off that night that you had some ideas on who it might be. I understand you don't want to stir things up by accusing people, but let's be honest: things are already quite stirred up here. I don't think that they're going to get stirred up that much more by your telling me what you might know. In fact, maybe it'll help calm things down if it helps me catch the murderer."

George took a long sip of his whiskey as he considered this. "You're probably right. I just hate to point fingers. What if I'm wrong?"

I chewed my lower lip. How could I get him to talk? Perhaps if I confessed to him all of my suspicions, then he might trust me with his. "I understand," I said. "Why don't I start by telling you what I've learned so far?"

George leaned forward with interest. "Okay. That sounds good."

Quickly, I told him about Jenny and the letters. Then I told him about Bruce's secret hiding place, and about how I thought there might be something in the building that would prove he had killed Big Al.

Apple Crumble Assault

George nodded sagely through all of this. When I finally finished, he went to refill his whiskey glass before speaking.

"None of that really surprises me. Like everyone else, my top three suspects all along have been Jenny, Tiffany, and Bruce. Honestly, I didn't think Jenny was the most likely culprit, but after what you told me about the secret hiding place, well...that seems a bit strange. I would say she's worth looking into a bit more."

"I'll definitely look into Jenny more, especially since you told me about the reality show. It sounds like she's going to gain from Big Al's death, which might mean she had a strong motive to kill him. But what are your thoughts? You mentioned there was someone in Sunshine Springs you suspected in particular?"

George still hesitated, so I decided to prod.

"Was it Bruce?" I asked. "I understand you wouldn't want to accuse such a prominent member of the Sunshine Springs community. But you must have your doubts about him, especially after hearing about his own secret hiding place?"

There was another long pause, and finally George sighed. "Yes, I think Bruce is the murderer. I don't have any rock-solid proof of it, but I had already heard things before you told me about his hideout that made me suspect that he was hiding something big. I had no idea just how big, but I knew he was hiding something. I didn't want to get him in trouble for no reason, but it sounds like maybe he deserves to be in trouble."

I nodded sadly. "Maybe he does. Don't worry. I won't tell anyone that you suspected him. I know you don't want people to think you're accusing anyone without a reason, and I know that you aren't just throwing around baseless accusations. I promise you I'll look more into this and let you know if I find more evidence against Bruce."

George thanked me effusively as I finished my glass of white wine. When he offered me a refill, I declined and said I should get going. I felt that now I had a clearer direction. If George also thought that Bruce was the guilty party, then I figured it was worth my time to focus on looking further into Bruce. Of course, I would still check into Jenny and Tiffany. But I couldn't deny that the fact that Bruce had a secret hideout behind an electric fence was suspicious.

As I was leaving his home, George asked me if I had actually talked to Tiffany yet.

"No," I answered. "I'm intending to, but I haven't had a chance yet. Why?"

George furrowed his eyebrow. "I just think it would definitely be worth talking to her as well. I've noticed that she's been retreating from the spotlight. Remember at the beginning of the week that she was in front of the news cameras almost every second? But for the last day or two, she's been hiding from the spotlight."

"Huh. You're right. I hadn't thought about it until you mentioned it just now, but it's true. I haven't seen anything of her for the last day or two."

George nodded. "It might just be that she's tired of the media circus. But maybe she's afraid of being caught, or feeling guilty?"

"Good point. I'll definitely check into her further."

George bid me goodbye, giving Sprinkles a few more exuberant ear rubs before we left. As I climbed into my car, I already felt better. I hadn't found any new suspects, true. But George had helped me to feel more confident than ever that one of my top three suspects—Bruce, Jenny, or Tiffany—had to be the murderer. I just had to flesh out which one it was. They all had motivation, and they all had evidence against them. I needed to build my case until I knew who had the most evidence against them, and who had actually done the deed.

As I started up my car, my phone started buzzing. It was then that I remembered that I still hadn't heard from Mitch, and I grabbed for my phone frantically, hoping the call was from him. But when I looked at the phone, it wasn't an incoming call making it buzz, but rather a calendar reminder. I slapped my forehead when I saw it.

"Oh, no! I totally forgot about this!"

Several weeks ago, Molly had begged me to come to a special gala at the library that was scheduled for this evening. She'd been working hard over the last few months to remodel the library and revitalize its collection of books, using funds that had been left to the library by one of Sunshine Springs' wealthy residents who had recently passed away. The gala tonight was intended to show off all that hard work, and to make people feel invested in their community library. Molly hoped that people would continue to donate even more money once they saw that the money from the recent windfall had been well-spent.

I couldn't believe I'd forgotten about the gala, but I thanked my lucky stars that I had at least had the foresight to put a reminder in my phone about it. Now, I had half an hour until it started, and I definitely was not dressed for the occasion. I was still wearing the same shirt and pants I'd worn at the café all day, and my hair was still up in a mess of a bun as it had been since about four o'clock that morning.

The last thing I felt like doing right now was going home, putting on a fancy dress, and doing my hair. But I couldn't miss this gala. Molly would kill me, and what kind of friend would I be if I didn't show up to support her at such a big event?

Sleeping would have to wait.

But maybe that wasn't a bad thing. Perhaps going to the gala would actually be helpful for me as I worked on this case. There were bound to be plenty of people from town there, and when large crowds from town converged in one spot, the gossip flowed freely. Perhaps I would overhear something that would shed some more light on the few clues I had already uncovered related to Big Al's murder.

You never knew what you might learn in a room full of Sunshine Springs' locals, and I was going to be all ears tonight.

CHAPTER FIFTEEN

I rushed home and took the world's fastest shower, then put my hair up into a neat, tight bun. I would have preferred to actually wash and blow dry my hair, then curl or flat iron it. But there was no time for that. I'd dropped the ball on remembering that this event was tonight, and if I took the time to really do my hair, I would be horribly late. I did at least put on some makeup, and I chose a sleek, black cocktail dress from my closet—a tasteful but gorgeous little number left over from the days when I used to attend networking cocktail parties as a lawyer.

I left Sprinkles at home with numerous apologies and a giant slice of pie.

"I promise we'll spend more time together tomorrow. I'm sorry to run off again, but I can't miss this event. And you know dogs aren't allowed at the library."

Sprinkles gave me the stink eye, and protested by refusing to take a bite of his pie. I wasn't worried, though. I knew as soon as he heard my car pull out of the driveway that he would break down and eat the pie. He was never too angry for pie.

When I arrived at the library, I could see that most of the gala's guests had already arrived. I saw a few locals going in dressed to the nines, and I felt suddenly nervous. I hoped that I was dressed fancily enough for this thing. But as long as Molly was happy that I was here and happy with the way I was dressed, I figured I'd be good.

As I got out of my car and approached the front door, I saw Scott walking in with a giant box in his arms. He was wearing a suit and tie, which I'd never seen before, and I couldn't help but laugh.

"All dressed up, and still hauling boxes around, huh?" I asked.

He glanced over at me and grinned. "Hey, Izzy. I can't seem to escape the boxes. But this isn't a delivery. Molly sent me to her car to get some napkins that she forgot. She's a total ball of stress, even though everything inside is gorgeous."

"I'm sure everything is great. But I'm not surprised to hear that she's stressed out. You know how much this event means to her."

Scott nodded. "Trust me, I know. She's reminded me about a thousand times today."

I followed him inside, thinking that it was a good thing that Scott was taking all of this in stride. Molly didn't get stressed out too often, but she'd been planning this event for a while and I knew it was taking its toll on her. Hopefully, it helped her that Scott was remaining steady and calm.

And hopefully, it would help her that I was here and calm.

Or, at least, I was going to *act* calm. I wasn't nervous about the gala, but I was nervous about other things. I would have loved nothing more than to pull Molly aside and share all the details of the sleuthing I had done over the last few days, but I knew this wasn't the right time for it. Once the gala was over, perhaps I could grab her and explain everything.

When I walked into the library, I couldn't help but gasp. It looked like the place had been turned into some sort of magical fairytale world. Soft, twinkling lights hung from the ceiling, and a space had been cleared in the lobby area for buffet tables and cocktail tables. Off to one side, a bartender stood behind a bar with beer and wine options. When I looked in that direction, I saw Mitch grabbing a glass of red.

My heart leapt at the sight of him. I hadn't really believed that something was wrong when he hadn't answered me all day, but I hadn't quite been able to shake a nagging feeling of worry.

Telling Scott I would catch him later, I made a beeline for Mitch, dodging around several fancily dressed couples as I did.

"Mitch!" I exclaimed. He turned at the sound of his name, and a smile spread across his face when he saw me.

My own heart skipped a beat at the sight of him. He was wearing a tuxedo, and while he always looked handsome, I had never seen him looking quite as sophisticated as he did in that moment. I frequently saw Theo in suits, but Mitch wore more casual clothes when he wasn't wearing his police uniform.

He cleaned up nice.

I knew that Theo wasn't coming tonight, because he was hosting another celebrity event at his winery. That was probably a good thing, because I wasn't sure I could have handled the sight of both Theo and Mitch wearing tuxedos at the same time.

I swallowed hard, trying not to let it show how much the sight of Mitch was affecting me. It was one thing to think Mitch was handsome. It was another thing entirely to let him know I thought that. He didn't need any encouragement in thinking that I might be interested in him.

Because at the end of the day, I wasn't interested in him. Not seriously, anyway. I was interested in looking, but that was about it.

"Good to see you, Izzy," Mitch greeted me, but he didn't sound very happy. He looked uncomfortable, and kept glancing around while taking long swigs from his wine glass. "These fancy events aren't my thing. I feel like an imposter wearing a tuxedo."

"Nonsense, you look great. But where in the world have you been? Why haven't you answered me? I've been trying to text and call you all day. You couldn't find two seconds to call me back?"

Mitch raised an eyebrow at me. "My phone is toast. I dropped it in a pond while trying to help one of the town's old ladies save her cat, which was stuck on a rock in the middle of the pond. I fished the phone out and put it in a bag of rice because one of my officers said that'll help dry it out, but I'm not holding my breath. I don't think the phone can be saved."

I shook my head sadly. "Yeah, I've tried the rice thing before and it didn't work."

Mitch shrugged. "It was just about time for a new phone, anyway. But if you needed to get in touch with me, you could have contacted me on the radio I gave you."

I slapped my forehead. "I completely forgot I had that," I said as I snatched a bacon-wrapped shrimp from a waiter walking by with a tray of hors d'oeuvres.

Mitch gave me a long-suffering look. "Really? You forgot you had the radio I gave you specifically so that you could contact me? Did you also forget about the bulletproof vest?"

I made a face at him. "No, but the vest is too big to wear around all the time. And as for the radio…I thought it was just for emergencies. This isn't exactly an emergency. I just wanted to talk to you about some new information I found on the case."

"Well, we can talk now," Mitch said grumpily. "Goodness knows I'd like something to keep my mind off the fact that I look completely out of place here."

"You don't look completely out of place," I insisted politely. "But yes, let's talk about things."

"But not too loudly," Mitch cautioned quickly. "I don't want the whole town to know all the details on this case. The last thing I need is someone leaking more information to the news media."

I nodded, and was about to start explaining to Mitch about Bruce's hideout and the letters Jenny had given me, when a loud voice screeched out my name.

"Izzy, darling! I didn't know you were coming tonight! You didn't look at all like you were planning on a gala when you dropped by to pick up Sprinkles earlier. I just assumed you weren't going to make it."

I looked up to see Grams rushing across the room toward me. Even though she'd interrupted me when I was trying to talk to Mitch, I couldn't help but smile. She looked striking with her turquoise hair, bright orange dress, and hot pink beaded necklaces. It was a crazy combination, but somehow she managed to pull it off with style.

"Grams!" I exclaimed as I greeted her with a hug. "To be honest, I forgot about the gala until a half-hour before it started. Don't tell Molly, but I almost missed it! I've just had a lot on my mind."

Grams winked at me. "Your secret's safe with me." Then she turned to look at Mitch. "And how are *you* doing, Sheriff. You look like your tuxedo's buttoned on a little too tightly."

Mitch tugged at his collar. "I think it is."

Before Grams or I could say anything else, another person was stopping by to say hello to Mitch. I waited as that person spoke to him, hoping that I would get a chance soon to finish my conversation with the sheriff. But with every minute that passed, the crowd around us only grew. Everyone wanted to ask Mitch about the status of the murder case, and the more he tried to downplay everything, the more questions people came up with. Soon, it became apparent that this gala was not going to be a good place to talk to Mitch about the case. As long as he was here in this building, he was going to be mobbed by members of the public demanding to know how things were going in the effort to catch Big Al's murderer. I watched as his expression grew more and more frustrated.

Everyone else was having a good time. Grams was laughing loudly, and across the room I could see that even Molly was smiling and seemed to be relaxing a little. But Mitch was clearly done with this party. He finally got two seconds to speak to me and quickly said, "This is never going to work. I need a chance to really listen to everything you have to say without being interrupted or without worrying that other people are going to hear. Can you meet with me first thing tomorrow morning? I can come by the pie shop. It's probably easier for me to sneak over there than for you to come to the police station. If the media sees you at the station too often they're going to figure out that you're helping with this."

I nodded. "Good point. Why don't you come by early, before the café opens? I'll be there baking pies, but I'll be leaving before the shop officially opens. One of your officers is helping run the place again tomorrow. He's actually really good at running a pie shop. I might try to steal him from you to use as a permanent employee."

I winked at Mitch, but he didn't find my little joke very funny.

"Don't you dare! I need all my officers to keep the city safe. You wouldn't want to be responsible for mayhem breaking out in Sunshine Springs because you stole away an officer to bake pie, would you?"

But then Mitch winked at me, and I was glad to see that his sense of humor was still a little bit intact. I started to reply, but I'd barely opened my mouth when he scurried into the crowd. He wasn't kidding about getting out of there. It amazed me how quickly a man of his size could move when he really wanted to get somewhere, and within moments he was slipping out the front door.

Once Mitch had disappeared from view, I turned my attention to the makeshift stage that had been set up for poetry readings. The readings were about to start, and Molly was asking everyone to take a seat. She looked gorgeous in a cocktail dress that matched the color of the sparkling champagne being passed around, and I felt a burst of pride at the sight of my best friend.

I settled into a chair next to Grams, eager to enjoy local poets as they read their original works. I tried not to think about the murder case as the poetry began, and I was actually quite successful at keeping my mind focused on the stage. I loved poetry readings, and this one did not disappoint. The poets had gone all out in an effort to put together beautiful words for this beautiful event.

The gala continued even longer than intended, with people sticking around to talk and laugh long after the official end time. But finally, everyone had cleared out except Grams, Scott, Molly, and me.

"Thank you so much for coming," Molly said as she came over to give me a hug. "And you, too, Grams. I've been a nervous wreck about this all week."

Grams gave me a mischievous side glance, and I knew she was making fun of me for having almost forgotten. Meanwhile, I was thanking my lucky stars that I had not, in fact, forgotten. Molly would have been devastated if I hadn't shown up.

"You must be exhausted, dear," Grams said to Molly. "Why don't you sit down and relax for a few minutes? The rest of us will start cleaning up."

"I agree," I said. "Have you even eaten, or have you been too busy running around taking care of everyone else? I'll put together a plate of food for you."

"I'm fine," Molly insisted. But Scott came over and joined us in insisting that she sit down.

"You might be fine," he said. "But you deserve to relax. Sit here and I'll turn the TV on for you. You can eat a little bit and catch up on the news while we clean up. I know you're dying to know the latest news on the Big Al murder case."

Molly groaned. "I've heard enough about that case to last me a lifetime. But I will take some food."

Scott got Molly a plate of food while Grams and I started cleaning up. And despite Molly's protests, Scott did turn on the news—although he kept the volume level low.

I glanced over at Scott. "If you want to hear about the case, then you should ask me about it."

Scott and Molly both gave me a sharp look.

"I thought you were done with sleuthing," Molly said.

"I thought so, too," I said. "But Mitch had other ideas. He asked me to take over the investigation. Unofficially, of course. But he actually wants me to work on this case."

Scott and Molly looked at me like I'd lost my mind. But Grams, who already knew what was going on, couldn't keep from chuckling.

"Funny how things change, huh?" she said. Scott and Molly still just stared at me.

I shrugged at them. "It's true. Mitch couldn't investigate properly because the media wouldn't leave him alone. They also were making him quite angry because they kept making fun of him for arriving at the scene of the murder wearing that ridiculous wrestling costume."

Scott burst out laughing. "You have to admit that costume *was* pretty funny."

"Oh, I'm happy to admit that it was funny. But Mitch isn't. He was livid about the whole situation, but it didn't matter how angry he was. The reality was that all the media was doing was stalking him and looking for another chance to make fun of him. He couldn't get anything done, so he handed the case over to me. Local people might realize that I've done some amateur detective work in the past, but the national news media has no idea. It's pretty easy for me to move around and look for clues without raising suspicion."

Molly shook her head in amazement. "Well, I'll be. I never thought I'd see the day that Mitch would actually want you to work on a case." Then, Molly leaned forward eagerly. "Well then, what have you learned? Give us the inside scoop!"

I grinned. "I was hoping you'd want to hear. I need more opinions on what I've found. Maybe you can help me make sense of all of this."

I'd been trying to keep things quiet so that I could talk to Mitch first, but I was tired of waiting on him. I wanted to tell my grandmother and good friends what I'd been up to for the last few days, so I described everything that had happened thus far in my investigation. Everyone was especially shocked by the fact that Bruce had a huge secret hideout outside of town, and they all made me promise to update them as soon as I found out what was actually hidden there. Molly was also quite interested in the letters that Tiffany had allegedly written to Jenny.

"That's funny," Molly mused as Scott poured her another glass of champagne. "Tiffany has actually been in here quite a bit over the last few days. She's been spending hours in the legal reference section of the library."

"Interesting," I said. "I wonder if she's worried about defending herself?"

Molly nodded. "I've been wondering that, too. Of course, just because she's trying to figure out how to defend herself, that doesn't mean she's actually guilty. I can't blame her for being worried with all of the accusations flying around."

I considered all of this. "It's obviously too late tonight, but I'll definitely go check on her tomorrow. She's acting suspicious if you ask me. Did you know that she's been pulling away from the news spotlight, too?"

"Really?" Molly asked. Then she frowned and nodded slowly. "I suppose she has. I'm still seeing Jenny on the news plenty, but now that I think of it, Tiffany hasn't been on in a few days. In fact, it's been a few days since I've even seen her here in the library. Maybe she's trying to lie low in hopes that this will all blow over."

I frowned, considering all of this. "Has anyone seen Tiffany *anywhere* in the last day or two?"

Molly shook her head. "I haven't. But that doesn't mean much because I've been mostly here, working like crazy to get ready for the gala."

"I haven't seen her either, come to think of it," Scott said. "She hasn't been around on any of the delivery routes I've been on."

I glanced at Grams with a questioning look in my eyes, but Grams shrugged and shook her head.

"I haven't seen her either, but that doesn't necessarily mean much. Sunshine Springs isn't *that* small. It would be possible to go a couple days without seeing her if you didn't happen to cross paths with her, or if she was hiding out in her home. And really, can you blame her for hiding out? Every time she steps foot outside her door the media tries to eat her alive."

"I suppose they do," I said. "Although, at the beginning she seemed to enjoy the attention. Maybe she just got tired of it and realized it's not all that exciting. Anyway, I'll check into it tomorrow and see if I can find her. Surely, she wouldn't have disappeared from town completely. She knows Mitch wouldn't want that, since she's technically a person of suspicion in this case."

"Well, if she did commit the murder and saw a chance to escape, why wouldn't she take it?" Scott asked.

I sighed. "True enough. I'll just have to wait until tomorrow to get more information."

"Okay, enough about the case," Grams said. "There's one more bottle of champagne, and instead of talking about such somber subjects, I say we share the champagne and celebrate the fact that Molly threw such a successful gala. I know it's going to help the library continue to become better and better for Sunshine Springs."

"That sounds like a good plan to me," I said. "I could use a bit of a break from the murder case. It's all I've been thinking about for the last day or two. Let's use this time to celebrate Molly and the library instead of rehashing everything about the murder case over and over."

No one was going to argue with that, so a few moments later we all had glasses of champagne in our hands.

"Cheers," Scott said. "To the most beautiful woman in the world, who has truly made this library a place that Sunshine Springs can be proud of."

He leaned over and gave Molly a kiss, and I couldn't help but whistle teasingly. Molly blushed, but she looked happy. It was still hard for me to believe sometimes that she and Scott were dating, but I loved how happy they were together. They balanced each other well, and Molly couldn't deny that she was enjoying being connected with the best gossip in Sunshine Springs, especially when there was a murder case going on.

For a moment, we were all silent as we took long sips from our champagne. During that silence, the news could be heard clearly even though the volume still wasn't turned up that loudly on the television. And it just so happened that during that brief moment of silence, Jenny herself came onto the news. I gasped as I heard the reporter introducing her.

And now, coming to you live from Sunshine Springs, where Big Al Martel was murdered, we have an exclusive conversation to share with you from Jenny Gullie, who will be starring in a reality show this fall about finding love after losing Big Al in such a tragic fashion. Tonight, Jenny has promised to share with us some exclusive news regarding the murder case.

Even though we had all just agreed not to talk about the murder case anymore, we couldn't help but turn our attention to the screen.

"What in the world," I said. "What is she going to talk about now?"

Beside me, Grams shook her head. "I don't know. But whatever it is, she looks quite pleased with herself. I'm not sure I've ever seen anyone looking so smug."

My heart sank as I looked up at the screen. Grams was right. Jenny did look quite pleased with herself. I gulped, and felt an uneasy feeling rising in my stomach.

I had a feeling that whatever Jenny was up to, it was no good.

CHAPTER SIXTEEN

I watched as Jenny approached the reporter's microphone. To my horror, I saw that she held photocopies of the letters she had given me earlier that day.

"What I have here," she said, as though she were explaining a painting at a fine art museum, "Is conclusive proof that Tiffany Glover murdered Big Al."

The reporter gasped in an overly dramatic fashion. I got the feeling that he had already seen the letters, but he was trying to give the impression that this was the first time they'd been shown to him.

"What exactly do you have here?" he asked, pausing to look at the camera for more dramatic effect.

Jenny went on to explain what the letters were, dramatically reading the last sentences of each letter, where Tiffany had threatened that if she couldn't have Big Al then no one could.

Molly gasped. "What is she doing? I thought she wanted you to take those to Mitch and keep them a secret."

I nodded as I looked at the screen. "That's what she told me earlier today. But apparently she's changed her mind."

Now, Jenny was telling the reporter that she'd taken the letters to the police, but that the police had done nothing and weren't taking this seriously. I moaned, and put my head in my hands.

"Great," I said. "Now Mitch is going to be furious with me! He's going to ask me why I didn't get this to him before she went on the air about it."

Molly reached over and squeezed my arm. "Don't worry about

that. He can't possibly be too mad, can he? You were trying to tell him tonight, but things were just too busy. And it's not your fault that he dropped his phone in a freaking pond so that you couldn't tell him earlier."

Scott snorted. "It might not be Izzy's fault, but that doesn't mean that Mitch isn't going to be angry at her. I've never seen him as on edge as he was tonight, and I don't think it was just because he was wearing a tux. I think this case is really getting to him. He doesn't like the fact that his town is in the national news, and he especially doesn't like that he has become the laughingstock of all the newscasts with the constant replay of him in his wrestling outfit."

I shook my head, unsure of what else to say. I gulped down the rest of my champagne, and decided then that it was time to call it a night.

"I better go home and get some rest. I have a feeling that tomorrow's going to be a long day."

Scott, Molly, and Grams nodded sympathetically.

"If there's anything we can do to help, let us know," Molly said.

I knew she meant that sincerely, but I didn't know what anyone could possibly do to help. I'd been feeling so much better about the case after today, but now I felt like things were getting out of control again.

Any goodwill that I'd felt toward Jenny had evaporated completely. How could she already be on the news saying she'd gone to the police when she'd only just given me the letters a few hours ago? Did she expect that Tiffany would have been arrested already?

I suppose she probably did. In Jenny's mind, Tiffany was unequivocally guilty, and should not be walking freely on the streets.

Was Jenny right about that?

I wasn't sure, but I *was* sure that Mitch was going to have an opinion about all of this. I glanced at my phone, half expecting to have a missed call from him already. But there was still nothing. I knew he had a landline phone at home, but perhaps he didn't have my number memorized and couldn't call me until he restored his contacts from the cell phone that he'd dropped into the pond. I was relieved that, for the moment at least, I was safe from having to talk to him.

I gave hugs to Grams, Scott, and Molly, and then got into my car to head home to Sprinkles. I'd have to be up early tomorrow. I had to make sure that I had plenty of time to get all the pies baked for the day, in addition to making sure that I had time to talk to Mitch in the morning. And now, I had a feeling that talking to him was going to take up more time than I'd originally thought.

But as I turned into my driveway, I saw that I actually wasn't going to have to wait until the morning to talk to Mitch. There, on my front doorstep, sat Mitch himself. He'd changed into a gray t-shirt and navy running shorts, and although the tux had been handsome on him, he looked much more like himself in the casual outfit.

But he still looked just as irritated as he had earlier in the evening—if not more.

"Mitch," I said cautiously as I climbed out of my car and headed toward my front door. That's when I saw Sprinkles' face in the front window behind Mitch. My pup was looking out, clearly confused as to why one of my best friends was sitting outside on my doorstep.

"What are you doing here?" I asked as I pulled out my keys to unlock the front door.

Mitch didn't exactly answer my question. Instead, he scowled at me. "I paged you on the radio several times. Why didn't you answer me?"

"I left the radio here. It didn't exactly fit in my evening purse."

Mitch let out a long, exasperated sigh. "If you're going to work on a murder case, you should make sure you have that thing with you at all times. You could have at least kept it in your car."

"Right. Of course," I said, not bothering to remind him that I'd already told him earlier that I'd forgotten about the radio. It's not like this was news to him. "Well, anyway. I'm here now. What did you want to tell me?"

"It's not so much that I want to tell you something. It's that I want to know why *you* didn't tell *me* about those letters. Is it true that Jenny gave them to you? I'm assuming that's what she means when she said she went to the police. If she'd gone to any of my officers directly, they would have paged me on the radio about it immediately."

I gulped. "She did give them to me, but just earlier this afternoon. I was trying to tell you about them at the gala, but we kept getting interrupted. I thought I'd show them to you when you came by the pie shop in the morning. I didn't realize she was going to go on the news tonight! She must have been planning this for a while."

Mitch sighed and cracked his knuckles as he followed me into the house. "Got any pie? I could really use a slice of something good to eat."

"I've got some strawberry moonshine pie. But didn't you have enough to eat at the gala? There was so much food there!"

I pulled the strawberry moonshine pie out of the fridge and set it down on my kitchen's island. Mitch grabbed a fork and started eating it before I could even get out a knife to cut the pie.

"Hors d'oeuvres aren't my thing," he said. "Now, tell me everything you know about the case. I don't want to be blindsided by anything else."

"Alright. Buckle your seatbelt."

With Sprinkles running in happy circles around Mitch's feet, begging for pieces of pie, and Mitch stoically shoving forkful after forkful of strawberry moonshine pie into his mouth, I told him everything I'd learned so far. I told him about Bruce's hideout, and he raised an eyebrow showing that he was surprised, but said little else. I explained to him about Jenny and the letters, and how she'd told me she didn't want me to tell him because of her secret hiding place. I figured that it didn't matter now if I told him where the letters had come from. Jenny had outed herself by going on the news, which I still couldn't wrap my mind around. She'd so adamantly said that she didn't want anyone to know where the letters had come from.

Mitch shook his head. "I don't know what Jenny is playing at, but my guess is that she just wanted to make you worry about telling me in front of too many people so that it would be harder for you to tell me. She wanted to get to the news before you got to me so that she could claim that the police knew and did nothing. She just wants a lot of attention."

I frowned. "You really think that's it? Seems like a lot of trouble to go to just for a bit more attention."

"Jenny is complicated. She's been twisting things around ever since this murder happened. She's trying to make it all about her, and she's come up with some pretty convoluted ways to do that. Part of me wants to think that she murdered Big Al just to get herself all this publicity. But in all honesty, I don't think she would have done that. I think that she was actually trying to capitalize on dating Big Al. I don't think she really loved him, but she liked the drama of being around him, and even the drama of fighting with Tiffany. Now, since Big Al is gone, that drama is obviously gone. But she's found a whole new source of drama. Jenny isn't completely dumb. She recognizes that the news cycle will eventually move on from Big Al's murder, so she's trying to milk this moment for all its worth and get herself a foot in the door in Hollywood."

Mitch let out a long sigh and looked up at me. "Was that it? Anything else I should know about?"

I shrugged. "I did also talk to George Drake, and he actually told me that he thinks Bruce is the guilty party."

"You got George to talk?" Mitch sounded surprised. "It's like pulling teeth getting him to say anything to my officers. He doesn't want anything to do with us. Try to keep him talking if you can. I think he knows a lot more about what went on behind the scenes in Big Al's life than he lets on. He just doesn't want to talk to us out of some weird sense of loyalty to Big Al, but I think the more he cooperates with us, the faster this murder will be solved."

I nodded. "I think you're right. I think he knows more than even he realizes, and his insights could really help us. I'll keep an eye on him and try to keep him talking. In the meantime, what are you going to do about Bruce and his hideout?"

"We'll have to get a warrant so we can go search the hideout. It'll probably take about a day or so, but I'm sure the judge will give me one. Don't say anything to anyone else about this, okay? If word gets out to Bruce that I know about his hideout, he might try to move whatever he's hiding to a different spot."

I winced. "Well, I already told Scott and Molly and Grams. But don't worry. They won't tell anyone."

Mitch groaned. "Sometimes you're so good at detective work, and sometimes you make me want to pull my hair out."

I shrugged and gave him a winning smile. What else could I do? Then, I shook a finger at him. "Don't act so high and mighty. You tell Theo everything. I know you do, because then he tells me."

Mitch couldn't deny that, so he just put another forkful of pie into his mouth. Then, he pushed the pie box toward me and straightened up. "I should go. I need to start working on that warrant request so I can have it to the judge first thing in the morning. Let me know if you find out anything else. I'll keep you posted on the warrant situation, but don't tell anyone else anything more than you already have, okay?"

"Okay," I said contritely. "I'll be good." Then I pushed the pie back toward him. "Keep it. You've made a mess of it anyway, and you'll probably need some more pie within the next day, the way things are going."

Mitch smiled at me. "Okay. Thanks. I won't come by the café in the morning then, but page me on the radio if you hear anything else. Or call me. I should have a working phone again by midmorning tomorrow."

"Okay. Will do."

From my front window, I watched him drive away while I ruffled Sprinkles' fur absentmindedly. Overall, that conversation hadn't been too bad. Mitch had been irritated, but not outright angry.

Once Mitch's rear lights were gone from view, I got ready for bed and went to sleep as quickly as I could. I had a feeling that the next day was going to be a big day, and I wanted to be well rested.

But it took me a while to fall asleep, and when I finally did, I had uneasy dreams. I woke several hours later with a start. My alarm hadn't gone off yet, but I thought that I'd heard my phone buzzing. Still in a daze of sleep, I looked over to see that I had several texts, all from Molly. Groggily, I unlocked my phone and started reading through the messages.

Izzy! Are you awake yet? I know it's a bit early, even for you, but I couldn't sleep and I started watching the news again. You won't believe what's happening now!

CHAPTER SEVENTEEN

Frowning, but suddenly feeling alert, I rolled out of bed and made my way to my living room. I quickly flipped on the TV, and saw that Jenny was on the news again, being interviewed in front of Tiffany's house. I only knew it was Tiffany's house because the reporter said so, but the interesting thing was that the reporter said that Tiffany wasn't there. Jenny was ranting about how Tiffany would not have had time to disappear if the police had taken her seriously from the beginning.

I frowned at the TV in confusion, then texted Molly back.

I just woke up. What in the world is going on?

I waited, and a minute later my phone buzzed with another text from Molly.

Tiffany is missing! The news is reporting that she's nowhere to be found, and that no one has seen her for several days. They're saying the police knew about it, which I'm not sure is true. But in any case, it looks like Tiffany might have made a break for it. That makes her look awfully guilty!

I stared at the TV, and soon heard the reporter saying everything that Molly had just told me. Now, I felt wide awake. I had a feeling that this was going to be a big day for this case. I bounded back to my bedroom and started to get dressed. Sprinkles looked at me like I had gone crazy, but I just shook my head at him.

"I know I look like a lunatic, but we have to get going. I want to get down to the pie shop and get started on the day's pies. The sooner I finish the baking, the sooner I can start working on this case again. I have to see if I can help find Tiffany. It looks like she might be the guilty party here!"

Sprinkles still looked at me like I was crazy, but I ignored his judgmental stare and quickly got ready to go. Less than fifteen minutes later, I was on my way to the pie shop with Sprinkles in the passenger seat beside me. As I drove, I turned the radio on to the news and heard the same report: that Tiffany was nowhere to be found. I shook my head, wondering if it was too early to try to reach Mitch and see what he thought of all of this.

But before I could make a decision on that, I was shocked when I stopped at a stoplight and looked out my window to see that George Drake was driving by.

I did a double take, and looked at the car again. It was definitely George's. I knew it well, because not many people in town were wealthy enough to drive a bright red Lamborghini.

George was heading in the direction of his neighborhood, but that couldn't be right. He was supposed to have flown to Los Angeles last night in preparation for the funeral today. Had he been held up? Was something else wrong with the funeral now?

"You know what, Sprinkles? Screw the pies today. I'm not going to sit around and bake when everything is falling apart with this case. I need to find Tiffany, and I need to go check on George and make sure he's okay."

Sprinkles didn't argue with me. I swung by the café and put up a "Closed for the Day" sign, then sent a quick message to the officer who was supposed to be working the morning shift to let him know he wouldn't need to bother coming in. With that done, I made my way to George's house.

But when I got there, it didn't look like George was home.

I got out of my car and went to ring the doorbell. Perhaps his car was already in the garage. The lights inside the house were out, and I wondered if he'd gone back to bed. I didn't want to disturb him, but I was also worried about him.

I rang the doorbell a few times, but there was no answer. George wasn't home. I looked down at Sprinkles and shook my head.

"He must have just been on his way to the airport or something. He probably got an early morning flight instead of a late night one. I'm going crazy with this case, seeing problems where there are none."

I turned to start walking back to my car.

"Come on. Let's go."

But Sprinkles wasn't interested in leaving. He barked at me, and I turned to look at him with an annoyed expression on my face.

"Come on. *Let's go*. He's not here. We rang the doorbell several times, and there are no lights on inside."

But Sprinkles barked again, and then, instead of following me to the car, he started running around the side of George's house.

"Sprinkles! What in the world are you doing?"

Sprinkles barked, stopped, looked back at me, and barked again. Then he turned around and continued running. With an exasperated sigh, I followed him. I didn't see that I had any choice.

As we rounded the side of the house, to my horror, I saw Sprinkles take a flying leap and jump over the fence into George's backyard.

My jaw dropped. I hadn't even realized Sprinkles could jump that high. The fence must have been six feet tall! I wouldn't have believed it if I hadn't just seen it with my own two eyes.

Sprinkles was trespassing in George's backyard. And now, I had no choice but to trespass as well. I had to go get my rascal Dalmatian out of there.

Looking uneasily over my shoulder, and hoping no one was going to see me and think I was trying to break into George's house, I followed my crazy dog into the inky blackness of the backyard.

What in the world was my crazy dog after?

Since, unlike my Dalmatian, I was definitely not capable of jumping a six foot fence, I was forced to awkwardly climb over. I had about as much grace as an elephant as I struggled to pull myself up onto the fence and then catapulted over.

I realized once I was in George's backyard that even though the gate couldn't be opened from the outside, it could be opened from the inside. That was at least one blessing in all of this. At least I'd be able to get out without risking life, limb, and dignity.

Once I caught my breath, I looked around to see where my rascal of a dog had gone. He was in the back of one of the flowerbeds, digging like crazy. My heart dropped and I hissed at him.

"Sprinkles! What's gotten into you? You can't just run around trespassing in people's yards and digging holes in their flowerbeds!"

Sprinkles ignored me and continued digging, forcing me to go drag him out by his collar. Even as I dragged him away, he whined in protest. In the quiet of the night, the sound was unnaturally loud, and my heart pounded in my chest from fear that we'd be caught back here. I looked around the perimeter of the fence and the house, worried that I would see a video security camera peering down at us. I didn't see anything, but that didn't mean there wasn't something there.

"Come on, Sprinkles," I insisted. He continued to ignore me, and I continued to pull him forcibly along beside me. "That's enough! The last thing I need right now is to have George angry with me on top of everything else."

Luckily, the yards here were so huge that it wasn't likely a neighbor would see me even if they happened to be looking out their windows at this moment—but I still didn't want to take any chances. I continued to drag Sprinkles out of the yard as quickly as I could. He whined the whole time, but I ignored him until we were all the way back in the front yard next to my car.

"I don't know what is wrong with you, or what you're trying to dig up back there, but this isn't a time for games. I don't care how tasty of a bone you think is in that flower bed: that's not our property, and we can't just barge into George's yard and start digging up his flowers."

Sprinkles hung his head, which I took to be as much of an apology as I was going to get from him. With a sigh, I opened the back door of my car and pointed to the back seat.

"Alright. In you go. I'm not letting you sit up front because your paws are covered with mud now. You can sit in the back until I have a chance to clean your feet."

Still hanging his head, Sprinkles took a step toward the car. But then he stopped and looked up toward the road with a bark.

I groaned. "What now?"

That's when I saw a car coming down the road. In the early morning darkness, all I could see were the headlights—but I was pretty sure just from that that it was George driving down the road. I gulped, hoping that he wasn't going to be in the mood to talk to me. There was no way for me to get out of there without his seeing me, but hopefully I could keep the conversation brief. Was he going to want details on why I was in front of his yard? Would he be able to see the guilt on my face and realize I'd been in his backyard?

He slowed as he approached his house. It was definitely him, and he rolled down the window to look at me with a confused expression on his face. "Izzy? What are you doing here so early in the morning? Is everything okay?"

I wasn't sure if I'd ever been so uncomfortable in my life, but I did my best to smile. "I'm fine. Sorry to disturb you at your home, but I saw you driving around town and I was worried about you because I thought you were supposed to already be gone for the funeral. I just wanted to make sure you were okay, so I stopped by. But when I knocked on the door you weren't home."

George frowned and glanced at Sprinkles. I sent up one thousand silent prayers that he wouldn't notice the dirt on Sprinkles' paws or question where it came from. George was silent for the span of about five seconds, but to me those five seconds felt like five years. Finally, he shrugged and shook his head sadly.

"I *was* supposed to be at the funeral today, but I'm not going anymore."

For a moment, I forgot to be self-conscious about the fact that I'd just been sneaking around his backyard. "You're not going to the funeral? But Big Al was one of your best friends!"

George nodded sadly. "I know. But I decided that the best thing I could do for his memory was not to go to his funeral."

I looked at him like he was crazy. "I don't understand."

George let out a long sigh. "There's been so much drama around this funeral, and everyone wants to be part of the publicity surrounding the event. People are fighting me on every detail, and threatening to make a big scene if I don't agree with them. I even had someone threaten me that they would sic security on me if I came to the funeral at all."

"What?!? Why would they do that?"

George gave me a defeated look. "Because they don't want me there giving my opinions on what should be done. As much as I care about Big Al, I decided that I don't want my presence to cause any hullabaloo at his funeral. So I decided to stay home. I'll raise a glass of whiskey to him here in private, and hope that if he is looking down on me he knows that I'm just trying to honor him the best way I know how."

As George finished speaking, he glanced at Sprinkles again. I couldn't be sure, but I thought he looked down at Sprinkles' paws. I told myself to be calm. It was perfectly reasonable for a dog to have muddy paws, right? There was no way George would magically know that the reason Sprinkles' paws were dirty was that the dog had been digging up George's flowerbeds.

Still, I couldn't get out of there fast enough. I did think that what George was saying about the funeral was a little strange. I certainly wouldn't have stayed away from my best friend's funeral because a bunch of lowlifes were trying to make a scene. But we all grieved in our own ways, and I didn't want to stand around questioning things anymore. I wanted to get out of there before George asked me any more questions about why I was there or why my dog looked like he hadn't had a bath in a month.

"I'm really sorry about all of that. It sounds like people are being awful to you. You'd think that in the wake of Big Al's death they would be kinder to one of his best friends, but I guess that's people for you."

George sighed. "I guess so."

I gave Sprinkles a nudge toward the car, and thankfully he got the point and climbed in. I quickly shut the door behind him so he couldn't change his mind and hop out again.

"Well," I said brightly. "I need to take off and get stuff done. But if you need anything at all, feel free to contact me. Even if it's just for me to come out and drink a glass of white wine with you while you have a glass of whiskey in Big Al's honor."

"Thank you," George said. "I truly appreciate that. Right now, though, I think I just want to be alone."

Fine by me, I thought. *I just want to get out of here.*

But out loud I said, "I understand. I hope you can rest and feel better about the situation. I'll leave you in peace, but do call me if you need anything."

I got out of there as quickly as I could. Sprinkles seemed to sense that he was in trouble, because he sat silently in the back seat as I drove away from George's house and to Tiffany's place as I had originally intended. But when I got to Tiffany's, the house was surrounded by news vans.

I promptly turned around. I didn't want to talk to the media, and I was pretty sure Tiffany wasn't going to come back while her house was surrounded like that. I had no idea where else she would have gone, though. I pulled over on the side of the road a few streets over to think. It seemed that I had reached another dead end. Where did I go from here? Tiffany was gone. I didn't think Jenny had anything else tell me, and I wasn't interested in talking to her after she'd pulled that stunt with the letters on me. Who did that leave? Bruce?

"We might as well look around outside his hideout again," I said to Sprinkles. "Mitch should be there sometime today with a warrant, and surely if I'm there he'll let me tag along on the investigation."

Sprinkles didn't answer me. He looked like he didn't dare make a peep of noise after how angry I'd been at him.

I shrugged, and started heading toward the outskirts of town. I actually wasn't entirely sure that Mitch would let me tag along on an investigation, but I had to try. I'd already committed to closing the pie shop for the day, so this seemed like a good alternative activity. I had to do *something* to keep moving forward on the murder investigation. Otherwise, the frustration over all the dead ends I was hitting was going to overwhelm me.

Besides, even though Tiffany was acting suspicious and disappearing, George still thought that Bruce was the most likely suspect as far as I knew. And there was no getting past the fact that a giant hideout protected by an electric fence did seem a bit suspicious.

As the sun began to rise, I turned my car to head toward that hideout. I had just driven into the heavily forested area that led toward Bruce's hideout when a flash of color in the trees caught my eye. I slowed down and squinted, but didn't see anything. Had I imagined it?

But then, I saw the flash of color again, and realized that there was a tent in the trees. Frowning, I slowed even more to take a look. Was someone squatting out here?

I'd regularly seen homeless people when I lived in San Francisco, but I had never seen a homeless person in Sunshine Springs. Perhaps that was because any homeless people out this way lived on the outskirts of the city? I wondered if I should report this to Mitch and see if he could do anything to help this person. Did the town of Sunshine Springs actually have any programs to help homeless people? And was I still technically within Sunshine Springs city limits? I might actually have gone beyond them at this point, but then which town was I technically in?

As all of these thoughts ran through my head, I saw another flash of color, this time in pink. The pink flash was moving quickly, and I realized that in addition to the tent, there was actually a person moving in the forest at the moment. I squinted through the trees, trying to see. But I must have lost track of where the person was, because I didn't see anything else. I was about to start driving off again, when the flash of color reappeared. For the briefest of moments, I saw the person clearly through the trees, and my jaw dropped.

"It's Tiffany!" I yelped as I threw my car into park, killed the engine, and bounded out of the car. Sprinkles barked excitedly and followed me out as I took off at a full run in pursuit of Tiffany Glover.

Perhaps my investigations today wouldn't all be dead ends, after all.

CHAPTER EIGHTEEN

"Stop!" I screamed as I ran through the trees. Branches scratched at my face, but I ignored them. I wasn't letting Tiffany get away.

Unfortunately for me, she was quite a bit younger and fitter than I was. I was having a hard time keeping up with her as she darted through the forest, completely ignoring my calls to stop.

Fortunately for me, though, she could not outrun Sprinkles. He bounded ahead of me, probably determined to redeem himself in my eyes, and he reached Tiffany within a matter of a minute. He grabbed on to the hem of her shirt with his teeth and refused to let go. When I caught up with him, she was screeching and trying to pull her shirt away from him.

"Get your dog off of me!" she screamed as tears started to run down her face.

"Alright, Sprinkles. That's enough." Sprinkles let go of Tiffany's shirt, but he didn't move too far away. He sat down and watched her with eagle eyes, looking quite proud of himself. I was pretty proud of him at the moment, too. I gave him a smile to let him know he was forgiven for his earlier transgressions, and he wagged his tail vigorously at me.

"You!" Tiffany exclaimed. "I should have known you would find me. You're always sticking your nose in Mitch's investigations."

I frowned at her. "Well, if you must know, Mitch actually asked me to help on this investigation. He was having a hard time getting anything done with the media following him around like a pack of wolves."

To my surprise, at that comment, Tiffany's face crumpled from an angry glare to a flood of tears.

"The news crews are horrible! They won't leave me alone! It was fun to be in the spotlight for about a day, but now I just want to get on with my life. I can't stand being chased by them. That's why I went into hiding."

My heart softened toward her a little bit. Her tears seemed sincere, and I wondered if perhaps she really was innocent and just caught up in all of this mess unwillingly. Of course, I had thought that Jenny seemed genuine, and look how that turned out. Unsure of how to proceed, I decided that if I acted kind toward Tiffany, she might at least trust me.

"I completely understand that you'd be over the media. Like I said, Mitch was, too. But surely, you understand that running and hiding makes you look guilty?"

Tiffany cried harder. "I know, but what should I have done? I'm not guilty! I don't deserve to be treated this way. Yes, I was mean to Jenny, and I'm ashamed of that. I shouldn't have acted the way I did, fighting with her and spitting in her face and all that. But she made me so mad, because I did love Big Al, and she didn't care about him at all. She just was trying to get his attention because she wanted to piggyback on his celebrity status."

I frowned, unsure of what to say. "But what about the letters?"

Tiffany looked up at me, her eyes wide. "Oh, no! Did she actually show the police the letters?"

My frown deepened. "Yes, she did. And I have to say that the threats you made in those letters sound awfully incriminating. You told Jenny that if you couldn't have Big Al no one could, and then a few days later he turned up dead! You realize what that looks like, right?"

I crossed my arms at her in an attempt to look tough.

Tiffany covered her face with her hands, as if trying to gain control of her emotions. She completely failed at that attempt.

When she looked back at me, she looked more upset than ever. "I know I never should have made those threats, but I can't take it back now. I didn't mean anything serious by it. I was just trying to get Jenny to back off. If I had known that someone was actually going to kill Big Al, then I would never have said those things." Tiffany dissolved into sobs that sounded like genuine grief. "I just loved him so much, and I couldn't stand the way Jenny was trying to take him from me for her own selfish gain. Now, I have no choice but to hide. Everyone thinks I killed him."

"I don't know that everyone thinks that," I said. "Most people probably think it was Bruce. At least, that's what they would have thought before these letters came to light. I don't know what people are thinking now."

Tiffany sobbed harder. "You see? I can't go back to town! Everyone thinks I'm guilty."

"If you're not really guilty, the best thing you can do is go talk to Mitch about this. Any help you can give him in finding the true murderer will be one step closer to clearing your name."

Tiffany shook her head sadly. "But I don't know who the true murderer is. I have no idea who would have actually killed Big Al. I just can't fathom how anyone would actually do something so horrible!"

I gazed intensely at Tiffany, trying to see whether she was telling the truth. Was she really as clueless about all of this as she claimed?

"What about Jenny?" I asked. "She's sticking her fingers in this case quite a bit. Do you think it's possible that she had something to do with his death?"

Tiffany frowned and considered this. "I thought about that a lot, but I honestly don't think she did. She was using Big Al, that's for sure. But I don't think she would have killed him. She's profited from his death, but he still probably would have been worth more to her alive than dead."

I wondered whether to ask Tiffany about Jenny's secret hiding place. I wanted to know if Tiffany thought that something in that secret hiding place might be related to Big Al's death. But Mitch hadn't even had a chance to talk to Jenny about the hiding place yet as far as I knew. Would he be angry with me if I talked to Tiffany about it?

I decided to go ahead and ask. Mitch might be angry, but I might not get another chance to talk to Tiffany about this. I had to know if she knew anything. Hopefully, Mitch would forgive me since I was doing this in the name of getting more information.

"Did you know anything about Jenny's secret hiding place? She said that's where she'd hidden the letters you sent her. She told me that she didn't go to the police earlier because she wouldn't be able to show them the letters without giving away her secret hiding place."

Tiffany didn't look at all surprised by this news. "Yes, I knew. I discovered her hiding place by accident. She uses it to hide drugs."

Tiffany said this as if it were no big deal, but my jaw dropped. "Jenny's doing drugs?"

Tiffany shrugged. "I don't know if she's actually doing drugs herself. But she's definitely selling them. You know how things go. You start mingling with the rich and famous, and you're bound to find someone who is involved in something shady like that. I found out by accident, and I threatened to go to the police if Jenny didn't leave Big Al alone. I was about to do it, too, but then Big Al died. After that, I knew that if I said anything about the drugs that Jenny would make the letters I'd written public, and I'd look guilty."

"But now she *has* made the letters public. What's to stop you from going to the cops about the drugs?"

Tiffany's lower lip trembled. "I don't care anymore what happens with Jenny. I hated her because she was trying to take Big Al from me. But Big Al is gone forever now. I don't want to involve myself in this case any more than I have to. I just want to move on with my life, even though I'm not quite sure how to do that. I regret writing those letters more than anything, but I hope that in time when the killer is found things will settle down and I can go back to normal life. In the meantime, I want to stay as far away from this investigation and the media spotlight as I can."

Now, I wondered if Jenny had killed Big Al to frame Tiffany. If Jenny had thought that Tiffany would reveal her secret, she would have needed a way to keep Tiffany quiet. Would killing Big Al and then revealing the letters have been her attempt at accomplishing that?

I was about to ask Tiffany what she thought of this, but before I could say anything, Sprinkles looked behind me and growled. I felt a chill run up my spine at the sound. His ears were flattening against his head, and he was pulling his lip back to show his teeth. Was there danger behind me somewhere?

I slowly turned, and that's when I heard the sound of heavy footsteps crashing through the trees. Every instinct within me said to run, but for some reason my feet wouldn't obey my mind. I heard a strangled sound from Tiffany's throat, and I knew she felt just as frightened as I did. Sprinkles started barking as we both stood frozen, looking into the trees and wondering who it was that was coming crashing toward us—and whether they were intending to hurt us.

This day was turning out to be full of surprises, and I could have done without any more of them. But like it or not, someone was coming through the woods toward me, and showed no signs of slowing down.

CHAPTER NINETEEN

"Izzy! And Tiffany?"

I recognized Mitch's voice seconds before he came crashing into view. I let out the breath I'd been holding in a rush of relief.

"Oh, it's just you."

Mitch did not look amused. "Just me? You should be glad that someone's looking out for you. I drove by your car on the side of the road and freaked out when I saw you weren't in it. I didn't know where you were, or if something had gone wrong. With a murderer on the loose, I can't be too cautious. I'm pulling you off this case. I never should've let you on in the first place."

"You can't do that! I'm just getting close to solving it. Look! I found Tiffany."

Mitch glanced at Tiffany, then back at me. "That's nice, but it doesn't make me feel better that you're here alone with a murder suspect. You're not even wearing your bulletproof vest! And where's your radio?"

He glanced down at my hip, where there definitely was not a radio clipped.

"Um, the radio's at home," I said sheepishly.

Mitch shook his head and grunted. "This was all a mistake. I let my own frustration over being made fun of by the news media cloud my judgment. I'm putting you in danger by having you on this case, and I'm not going to do it anymore."

Mitch pulled his radio off his belt and paged the police station. "Officer Smith? Yeah, can you come down to County Road 722? I'm going to need you to escort Izzy and Tiffany back to Sunshine Springs."

"Tiffany? Tiffany Glover?" Officer Smith's voice squawked over the radio.

"Yes, Tiffany Glover."

"Roger that. I'll be there in less than ten minutes."

Mitch put his radio back on his belt, and turned toward Tiffany and me. "Come on, both of you. Move. Let's head back to the road."

I made a face at Mitch as we walked, but he ignored me and turned toward Tiffany. "I'm assuming that's your tent a little ways up there?"

She glared at him. "There's no law against camping, is there?"

Mitch ignored the question, choosing instead to say, "I don't know what's going on here, but you do know that the fact that you disappeared makes you look awfully guilty, don't you? And, if you haven't heard, we've come across some letters that look pretty bad for you."

"She has heard," I said. "I told her. I also learned some information about Jenny from her that you might be interested to hear."

Mitch glanced back and forth between Tiffany and me. "I'll need statements from both of you. But that will have to wait until I can get back to the station. Right now, I need to get to Bruce's hideout. I finally got the warrant, and I want to get that place searched sooner rather than later. Who knows what evidence Bruce might already have hidden because we didn't know about the hideout in time!"

"You're going to the hideout?" I squeaked. "I want to come, too! You can't just shut me out all of a sudden like this! I found all these clues for you, and now you're going to force me to sit on the sidelines just when things are getting exciting?"

Mitch sighed. "It's for your own good. I don't want you to get hurt, and I was a fool to think I could put you on this case without exposing you to danger."

I turned and frowned at him. "Just let me come with you. I won't be in danger if you're with me. Besides, I wasn't really in danger here. Tiffany isn't going to hurt me, and I had Sprinkles with me to protect me."

Mitch gave me an annoyed glance and cracked his knuckles, but kept walking without saying anything else. I sped up to hurry after him.

"Come on," I pleaded. "You want to hear what I have to say about Jenny, don't you? I can tell you on the ride over to the hideout. That way you don't have to wait for an official statement."

Mitch turned to glare at me again, and for a moment I was sure that he was going to tell me off again. But then, to my surprise, he grunted and nodded.

"Fine. You can come with me. But you have to promise me you'll do exactly as I say. If I tell you to stay somewhere, you need to stay. If I tell you to wait in the car, you need to wait in the car. No arguing, do you understand?"

I nodded quickly. "I understand. I promise I'll listen."

My heart leapt, and I kept my mouth shut for the rest of the walk back to the road, worried that if I said anything at all that Mitch would be annoyed with me and change his mind.

By the time we got back to the road, Officer Smith was pulling up. Mitch handed Tiffany over to him, telling him to take her back to the station and get a statement. As for me, I climbed into Mitch's police cruiser, and Sprinkles hopped into the backseat. A few minutes later, we were pulling up to the spot where Bruce's secret hideout was located. There were a few other police officers there already, along with Bruce himself—who did not look happy.

"Bruce is here, too?" I asked. I instantly felt self-conscious, and thought that perhaps I shouldn't have shown up. Bruce was looking at me like I had betrayed him. Did he know that I was the one who had found this place? But then, I pushed away these thoughts. I shouldn't be feeling badly. If Bruce was hiding something illegal, that wasn't my problem. I had no duty to protect a murderer, and I wasn't going to feel badly for telling the police what I'd found here.

I held my head high as I got out of the car. Sprinkles followed me, and Bruce shook his head at me.

"I can't believe this," he said to me through clenched teeth. "I thought we were friends. I didn't have anything to do with the murder. I hated Big Al, but I'm not a killer. Nothing on this property has anything to do with Big Al's death!"

"Enough," Mitch said. "If you have nothing to hide, then you shouldn't be worried about showing us this place."

"I have nothing to hide about the murder," Bruce said angrily. "But this is my private property. What I have here is personal."

Apple Crumble Assault

Mitch clearly wasn't in the mood to argue. His eyes darkened as he turned to Bruce. "Open the gate. You've seen the warrant, and if you make this hard on us then things are just going to be worse for you. Let us in and cooperate, and I'll do my best to go easy on you."

Bruce sighed. "I haven't done anything illegal, so I don't need anyone to go easy on me. But I guess you're not going to believe that until I show you, and I can't argue with the warrant. But this is personal, okay? What you see here is between us."

Mitch shrugged. "If there truly isn't anything illegal here, then whatever your secret is, it's safe with me."

Bruce grunted, seeming mildly appeased by this. I held my breath, thinking that he was going to demand that I couldn't go in. But he didn't seem to realize that I wasn't officially a police officer. I guess he was too worried about whatever it was he was about to show us to think about details like that. I kept my mouth shut and tried to be as inconspicuous as possible. That wasn't easy to do with Sprinkles tagging along beside me, but thankfully Bruce seemed too upset with the whole situation to think about me much.

A few minutes later, we had all piled back into the police cruisers and were driving down the gravel road toward the building inside Bruce's hideout. Bruce got out and entered a code into the keypad to unlock the door, looking miserable as Mitch and the officers silently walked into the building.

As I walked past him, he put his head in his hands, muttering dejectedly. "I'm ruined. This is worse than the food poisoning incident. At least that scandal wasn't actually true. But this…this is going to ruin me!"

I frowned, and turned to look at him. Was he saying that he was the murderer, or was this something else entirely? I felt badly for him, which didn't make sense if he was about to be found out as a murderer. But he looked so miserable in that moment, and although we had never been super close, I did think of him as one of the most prominent members of Sunshine Springs. It was hard to reconcile my view of him as an important Sunshine Springs local with the idea that he was actually turning out to be the murderer.

But if he was indeed the murderer, then he didn't deserve my sympathy. I turned away from him to follow Mitch into the small building that held Bruce's secrets.

When I got inside, though, I was confused at what I saw. There

Apple Crumble Assault

were trees everywhere, just like I'd thought that first night when I'd found the place. It appeared this was some sort of strange, giant greenhouse, but why in the world would Bruce have a building full of trees? And why was he so secretive about it?

From the looks on the police officer's faces as they moved through the rows of trees, they were just as confused as I was. Finally, Bruce's voice rang out across the room.

"Truffles," he explained wearily.

We all turned to look at him.

"Huh?" Mitch asked.

"Truffles," Bruce repeated. "Black truffles grow on the roots of certain trees. You can grow them indoors, although it's not easy to do. That's what this is: an indoor truffle farm."

I flashed back to the dinner I'd had in his restaurant with Theo, and remembered Theo saying that Bruce wouldn't share his French truffle supplier with anyone, no matter how much people begged. Suddenly, everything clicked into place.

"Your restaurant!" I exclaimed. "The truffles aren't really from France, are they? You grow them here. Your 'supplier' is actually yourself."

Bruce nodded, tears glistening in his eyes. "I never intended for things to get this out of hand. But when I first started serving the truffles in my restaurant, a restaurant critic called them the best French truffles he'd ever tasted. After he said that, my restaurant really took off. I never lied to him about it. He just assumed they were French. But then, I was afraid that if I told people that the truffles weren't from France but were actually grown right down the road, that my restaurant would go under. So there you have it. This whole hideout has been set up to keep my truffles secret."

We all stared at him, not sure what to say. Finally, I threw my hands in the air in exasperation. "I don't understand. Your truffles were really good. Why would anyone care where they actually came from as long as they tasted good?"

Bruce shrugged. "People are weird about their truffles. I just wanted to make a success of my restaurant, and this seemed like the best way to do it. I couldn't tell anyone the truth, especially after that whole food poisoning incident."

Bruce hung his head in shame, but neither Mitch nor his officers looked like they could have given two hoots about where his truffles came from.

"Alright," Mitch said with a sigh. "Wrap it up. Let Bruce close up his truffle house, and let's get back to the station. Clearly, this place doesn't have any murder evidence to be found."

Bruce remained silent as he closed up the building and climbed back into his car. I wanted to say something comforting to him, but I had no idea what words might make him feel better. Clearly, I wasn't well-informed about the world of truffles. I thought it was no big deal that Bruce's truffles didn't come from France, but from the look on Bruce's face, you'd think that his life was over. Could it really be that bad for his restaurant that his truffles came from just down the road? I wanted to ask him about it, but I could tell that he definitely wasn't in the mood to talk.

Mitch kept silent on the ride back to my car, looking immensely frustrated. I'd already told him everything I knew about Jenny and Tiffany, and he told me he'd have some of his officers look further into the possibility that Jenny was selling drugs. Since Bruce now appeared innocent, Jenny currently seemed like the most likely suspect. If she'd had some sort of drug operation going that Big Al was threatening to expose, perhaps she would have killed him to keep him silent. I wasn't an expert on the world of drugs, but I knew selling drugs could be big money—and money could definitely motivate people to murder.

Just as Mitch pulled back up to my car, I got a text from Molly.

OMG, just saw Tiffany! Apparently she's back!

I was about to text her back and explain as quickly as I could that I'd already seen Tiffany, but then Mitch's radio squawked. It was one of his officers, telling him that Tiffany had fled the police station.

Mitch banged his fist on his dash. "What?" he roared into the radio "I thought I told you to keep her there until I could get back and get a new statement from her!"

"I know," the officer's voice squawked over the radio. "But she completely faked us out. She acted super-cooperative, and I went to get her some food because she told me she hadn't eaten in a few days. I didn't handcuff or lock her in because she seemed to be so willing to stay and help us. Besides, she wasn't actually under arrest yet, so what could I do? But when I came back, she was gone. The receptionist didn't see her walk out, so she must have snuck out the back."

"I can't believe this!" Mitch roared. "Send some officers out to look for her. We have to find her! Bruce isn't the murderer, and from the way Tiffany has been acting, I'm starting to think maybe she is!"

My eyes widened, and I quickly texted Molly back. *Where are you? Do you still have eyes on Tiffany? The police are looking for her!*

I got back a quick, cryptic text a few moments later. *Was drinking coffee on a patio on Main Street when I saw her. Getting in car now to follow her and will update as I can.*

"I can't believe this," Mitch roared again. He was driving up beside my car now, but I shook my head as he slowed down.

"No time for that," I said. "Let's head back into town. Molly has eyes on Tiffany."

Mitch looked at me like I'd gone insane, and I held up my phone as if that explained things. He still looked at me like I was crazy, so I tried to explain further.

"She's texting me. She just saw Tiffany, and she's going to follow her to see where she's going."

Mitch exhaled, then reached up and switched on his lights and siren. "What a day," he said, and then took off at full speed toward Sunshine Springs.

CHAPTER TWENTY

"Where is Tiffany heading?" Mitch demanded.

"She hasn't sent me an update," I said as I stared down at my phone, willing Molly to text me. "She's probably driving, so it wouldn't be easy for her to text."

"Call her then!" Mitch said. "I have to know where to find Tiffany. She must be the murderer if she's running again!"

Tiffany hadn't seemed all that murderous to me, but the fact that she was running once more did look suspicious. I was about to dial Molly's number when I received another text. I nearly jumped out of my skin as my phone buzzed, but I took a deep breath to calm down as I silently read the text.

Tiffany just parked in front of George Drake's house! She's going up to the front door!

"George!" I said aloud. "Why would she go there?"

"George Drake?" Mitch exclaimed.

I looked over at Mitch, feeling just as bewildered as he sounded. "That's what Molly said."

Mitch swung his police cruiser in the direction of George's neighborhood. In the backseat, Sprinkles barked excitedly. He loved the excitement of all of this. I'm sure it was much more thrilling for him than spending the day cooped up in the back of the pie shop like he often did.

It felt like it took an eternity to get to George's house, but it must only have been about three minutes. By the time we got there, George was out on his front lawn, and Tiffany was yelling at him.

Molly stood just outside of her car, watching them with her mouth gaping open. Mitch swerved into a screeching halt in George's driveway, then hopped out of his police cruiser just as Tiffany launched a punch at George's face. George deflected it, but Tiffany kept trying to punch him.

"Thank God you're here," George yelled. "Get this crazy woman away from me!"

Mitch went to try to pull Tiffany away from George, while Sprinkles and I got out of the car and headed over to Molly.

"What's going on?" I asked.

"I don't know, exactly," Molly said. "But it sounds like George misled Tiffany about which day Big Al's funeral was going to be."

"The funeral's today, isn't it?" I asked.

Molly nodded. "Yup. The news media has been covering it all day. But somehow Tiffany just figured out that it was today, and she's yelling at George that he gave her the wrong day."

I looked over to see Mitch pulling Tiffany back and trying to call for backup at the same time. I went over and took his radio from him.

"Allow me. I do know how to use this thing, even though I never bring mine with me."

I paged the police station and asked for a few officers to come down to George Drake's house to arrest a murder suspect. Tiffany went through the roof when she heard those words, nearly getting out of Mitch's grasp.

"I'm not a murderer! How many times do I have to say it? I loved Big Al! Can you blame me for being angry that this idiot here gave me the wrong day for the funeral?"

"Of course I gave you the wrong day!" George spat out. "You and Jenny are just horrible gold diggers trying to get money from him and using his celebrity status for your own gain!"

I had never seen George acting quite so venomous, and it surprised me a bit. But I knew he hated both Tiffany and Jenny, so I supposed it wasn't that unexpected.

"Oh, *I'm* a gold digger?" Tiffany said. "What about you? Acting like you're actually friends with him just so that he'll invest in your businesses? He wasn't an idiot, you know? He knew you still hated him!"

I frowned at this. George was yelling again, but I ignored him and looked at Tiffany. "Wait a minute. What did you just say? I thought George and Big Al were really close?"

Tiffany looked at me and laughed. "No way. George wanted everyone to believe that. He even tried to convince Big Al that he wasn't still mad at him about the fact that Big Al had gotten all the good parts back in the theater days. But Big Al knew it was all just a ruse. He went along with it because he needed business advice from George. He was also afraid that if he wasn't nice to George that George would shut him out of Sunshine Springs."

"I'm so confused," Mitch said. "George and Big Al weren't actually friends?"

"We *were* friends!" George exclaimed. "Why do you think he trusted my judgment that Sunshine Springs was a good place to invest?"

Tiffany let out a bitter laugh. "He trusted your judgment on business investments here because you know the business market. But that doesn't mean you two were friends. You were both just trying to make money off of each other. I told Big Al not to work with you. I told him to try to do it on his own. He didn't need your help, but for some reason he was convinced that he did. He thought that if you told everyone in Sunshine Springs not to do business with him, that he wouldn't be able to get a foot in the door here."

"That's sort of true," I said. "It *is* hard to start a business here without the support of a local. I know that from experience, because I had a hard time getting my café going even though my Grams is a local and is well loved by the community. If George had said spiteful things about Big Al, it would have been nearly impossible for Big Al to get any businesses going here, no matter how much of a celebrity he is."

Tiffany shrugged. "I don't know. I'm not a businessperson and I don't know much about how business here works. But I do know that George and Big Al weren't friends. George was still holding a grudge over a play they were both in ten years ago. Big Al got the lead, but George got a crappy part and he hated Big Al for upstaging him."

"You're out of your mind," George said angrily. "You're making up stories to try to make me look bad, but you were the one just after his money and fame."

Tiffany snorted. "Yeah, right. Want to tell everyone the real reason that you weren't at the funeral? Nobody wanted you there, because everyone knows that you and Big Al hated each other. Of course, they don't know exactly why. But I do. Big Al told me all about how you hated the costume you had to wear in that play ten years ago, and that you thought you would have done a much better job in the lead role than him."

I frowned as I listened to Tiffany. "Wait a minute. They got into a fight over a specific play that George had to wear a strange costume for?"

Tiffany shrugged. "That's what Big Al told me. He even admitted to me that he probably made fun of George's costume more than he should have, but that he couldn't help it because it was just so funny when George couldn't even walk straight in the thing."

"Oh my god," I said, turning toward George. "It was you, wasn't it?"

Mitch and Molly both looked at me like I'd lost my mind, and George shook his head at me. "Izzy, you're being delusional. You're not actually going to believe what this crazy woman's telling you, are you?"

In response, I ran across the front yard and into George's house. Thankfully, he'd left the door unlocked. I ran into his living room and prayed that he hadn't bothered to put the photo album away yet. My heart sank when I realized it was gone. Frantically, I looked over all the spines of photo albums on the bookshelf, desperately trying to find the one that he hadn't wanted me to look at the first day I was there. But it was gone, which only made me even surer that it had photos in it that would explain everything.

I could hear George yelling and running in behind me. "Get out of there! This is my private property! What are you doing just running in here and going through my things?"

He ran into the room with Mitch running after him. I saw George's eyes darting toward his whiskey cabinet, and that's when I knew: that's where he'd hidden it. I dove for the whiskey cabinet and flung the door open.

Inside, I found the photo album.

"Hey! Leave that alone!"

I ignored George, grabbed the photo album, and ran as fast as I could back out to the front yard, where I found several police officers had arrived now and were trying to handcuff Tiffany.

"Leave her alone!" I said. "It wasn't her."

Mitch and George were running back after me, George tried to tackle me, but he missed and tripped, falling face-first onto the plush green grass of his lawn. "Stop! I forbid you to open that! It's private property!"

I ignored him, and threw the book open. Quickly, I flipped the pages. The first few pages looked like rehearsal photos, and no one was in costume. But when I reached the photos of the actual play that George and Big Al had been in, I saw confirmation of what I had feared.

Big Al was in the photos, wearing a striking, sophisticated costume that made him look like a wealthy prince. Meanwhile, on the opposite page, there was a photo of a man in a monkey costume. It was a full costume, so it was impossible to tell who was inside the furry fabric. But I would have been willing to bet it was George. In big red marker on the pages of the photo album, someone—presumably George—had written "You'll pay for this!" under the picture of the monkey costume.

"What is this?" Mitch asked, looking down at the monkey costume photo.

"I think I just found your murderer," I said as I looked at George. "You wanted revenge, didn't you? You told me that you were embarrassed by these photos, and that was true. But it wasn't just a lighthearted, good-natured embarrassment. You've been angry about this for years, and you've been biding your time until you could get back at Big Al for the fact that he got the good part in that play and went on to become a celebrity while your acting career never got any further than being a monkey in a costume."

George glared at me. "I don't know what you're talking about! Big Al and I were friends. It's just coincidence that I was a monkey in that play. It doesn't have anything to do with the murder!"

Tiffany snorted. "Get real. You guys weren't friends. Sure, now and then you did act friendly toward Big Al. He told me that you would call to say you'd had a change of heart and wanted to be friends again, and that you even went on vacations together a few times. But in the end you would always give in to your hatred toward him and try to hurt him."

"I was a true friend to him, but he used me! He went and auditioned for that show behind my back. I should've had the lead, but he swooped in at the last moment and took it from me, relegating me to that stupid monkey costume. Now, he was trying to take away my place as a top businessman in Sunshine Springs. But I wasn't going to let him! He may have beaten me at acting, but he never could have beaten me at business."

"I'm so confused," Molly said. "Did you or didn't you kill Big Al?"

I glanced over, surprised to see she was still standing there amidst the officers.

"I didn't kill Big Al!" George exclaimed.

But at the same moment, Tiffany yelled, "I'm sure he did."

George glared. "Look, it's true that Big Al and I weren't always the best of friends like I try to make everyone believe. But we were trying to patch things up between us. We may have had our differences, but I didn't murder him! I would never do that!"

I looked over at Mitch, who looked uncertain.

"I think perhaps you should come down to the station and give a statement," Mitch finally said.

George looked up at him angrily. "What? Why? Don't you believe me? I didn't kill him, I swear!"

Mitch raised his hands up in a gesture of surrender. "Look, if you didn't, then there is no need to be so upset. Just come give a statement so that we have it on record. It's just a formality whenever someone is tangled up in a murder case, and unfortunately it looks like you've gotten yourself a little tangled here."

"I didn't do it!" George roared. "This is an outrage!"

"Hey! Izzy!" one of the Police Officers suddenly interrupted. "What's your dog doing?"

I looked around, realizing that Sprinkles had disappeared. In all the excitement, I'd forgotten about him. But now, I looked over in the direction the officer was pointing and saw Sprinkles prancing across the yard toward us. His legs, paws, and muzzle were covered in dirt, and he was dragging along a muddy mess of fur that looked suspiciously like a monkey costume.

"What in the world?" Mitch asked. "What's he got there? And where did he get it?"

My jaw dropped open. "You knew, didn't you?" I asked Sprinkles. Sprinkles dropped the costume and barked happily.

"He knew what?" Mitch asked.

I turned to look at Mitch. "Earlier today, I came by here with Sprinkles to check on George. George wasn't here, but Sprinkles went crazy and jumped into the backyard and started digging a hole. I thought he was just being a crazy dog, but he must have known that there was a monkey costume buried back there! He was trying to show me, but I thought he was just digging holes, so I dragged him away. If your officers go look in the flower bed right now, I'm sure they'll find a hole in the ground about the size of this monkey costume."

Molly and Tiffany both stared at Sprinkles with their mouths gaping open.

Then, tears started rolling down Tiffany's face as she turned to look at George. "It *was* you! I really didn't want to believe it, but it's true, isn't it? You killed the love of my life. I hope you rot in jail forever for it!"

Then, she buried her face in her hands and started sobbing. The police stood uncertainly around, looking to Mitch for guidance, until George couldn't take it anymore and literally spat in Tiffany's direction.

"Oh, get over it. He was a jerk and you know it. You're better off without him, and you should thank me for removing him from your life."

My jaw dropped open again. George had basically just confessed to the murder, a fact that definitely wasn't lost on Mitch. Shaking his head, Mitch stepped forward and reached to pull George's hands behind his back.

"George Drake, you're under arrest for the murder of Big Al Martel."

George howled in protest, and several of the police officers moved to help Mitch subdue the suddenly angry George. Meanwhile, Sprinkles marched proudly over to me, and I looked down at him with a smile on my face. "I guess I owe you an apology, huh?"

He woofed in reply, looking quite pleased with himself.

"Would you take some pie as an apology?" I asked him. He woofed again, and I laughed, then ruffled his ears. "Alright, pie it is."

Molly grabbed me then, pulling me close to her with one arm and pulling her cell phone out of her back pocket with the other.

"Come on!" she said. "Quick! Let's get another selfie for my album of selfies with murderers being arrested in the background."

I laughed. "I should've known that was coming. I thought these days were over after the last murder case. But I guess, thanks to Mitch needing my help, you'll get one more photo for the ol' murder selfie album."

Molly snapped a photo of us and then laughed.

"This might not be the last one. You seem to have a way of getting yourself involved in all sorts of things, no matter how much you try to stay out of them."

I glanced back at George, who was fighting as hard as he could now. But he couldn't overcome the five or so officers that were holding him back.

"You're right," I said. "But I at least hope this is the last one for a while. Sunshine Springs deserves a little bit of peace and quiet after all of this ruckus."

Mitch must have overheard me. "Yes, it does," he called over. "And thanks to you, we might actually have that."

I winked at him. "We might. But I'm keeping that bulletproof vest and radio, just in case."

Then, I turned and ran off before he could argue with me about that.

Hey, an amateur sleuth deserves a little souvenir now and then, right?

CHAPTER TWENTY-ONE

Two days later, the news media and celebrities were slowly starting to seep out of Sunshine Springs. After the story of George's betrayal of Big Al broke, it had dominated the news for about twenty-four hours. But then, people started to lose interest, and our little town once again became a peaceful, relaxing place to live.

Things had moved slower at the Drunken Pie Café today, which wasn't a bad thing. I was happy to have a bit of a breather both from chasing down a murderer, and from running around like crazy serving pie. The day had been busy, but not overwhelmingly so. I'd sold some pie and made some money, but I hadn't had to run myself ragged.

I'd also had time to bake a few pies for a special order for Theo. He'd scheduled one final celebrity event at his winery tonight, and he'd asked me if I'd be willing to cater dessert for the party. I honestly hadn't felt like baking extra pies, but Theo had sounded desperate, and he was a good friend. So I baked a few apple bourbon crumbles and a few death by chocolate pies for him. I also agreed to deliver them directly to the winery. I didn't often make deliveries, but again, Theo had sounded desperate. Besides, I didn't have anything else to do, and it might be interesting to see which celebrities were actually still hanging around our little town.

I brought Sprinkles along with me, and drove directly to the winery after closing the pie shop down. I was a bit surprised to find the parking lot completely empty. I didn't even see any cars from Theo's employees.

"That's weird," I mused aloud. But perhaps it was still some time until the party started. I got out of the car and stacked all my pies carefully in my arms, then headed to the front door, praying I'd be able to open it without dropping the pie boxes everywhere. Sprinkles followed me, and I didn't bother telling him not to head into the winery. He wasn't allowed in there during business hours, but business hours were passed, and clearly Theo's special celebrity event hadn't started yet.

Thankfully, when I reached the front door, it had been left unlatched and open just a crack. I kicked it open with my foot, hardly able to see past the stack of boxes I held.

"Hello?" I called as I wriggled into the tasting room. "Anyone around? Theo?"

"SURPRISE!"

I shrieked, and nearly dropped the pie boxes as all of a sudden at least twenty Sunshine Springs locals leapt up from behind the tasting room's counter. Thankfully, I managed to hold on to the boxes—much to Sprinkles' disappointment. He would have loved the chance to "clean up" dropped pie.

As I recovered from my shock, I realized that the tasting room was decorated with balloons, streamers, and a giant banner that read "Happy Birthday Izzy." I saw Theo standing in the middle of the crowd of people behind the counter, and I realized that this was definitely not a celebrity event. This was a hometown event, filled with the people I loved most in the world. In addition to Theo, I saw Grams, Scott, Molly, and Mitch. My friend Alice from the Morning Brew Café was there, as was Moe from Moe's souvenir shop. Even Tiffany was there, looking lovely in a green party dress—and looking decidedly less stressed out than the last time I'd seen her.

As my eyes scanned the group, I saw several more faces of people I'd become friends with over my short time in Sunshine Springs. Everyone smiled back at me expectantly, as though waiting for me to say something. I looked up at the "Happy Birthday" banner, and then looked back down at Theo.

"What's going on? This doesn't look like a celebrity party."

He waved a hand dismissively. "No, of course not. The celebrities are all gone now, thank goodness. I just made up that story to get you out here without raising your suspicions. This is your surprise birthday party!"

I frowned, still feeling confused. "But my birthday isn't for another week."

Grams, who was wearing an electric purple blouse and hot pink jeans, stepped forward. "Of course your birthday is a week away. What better time to surprise you with a party." She laughed. "From the look of shock on your face when you walked in, I'm guessing you didn't suspect a thing."

I smiled as I slowly started to understand that this actually was a surprise birthday party for me. "Wow. Thank you, everyone. I was definitely shocked. In fact, I almost dropped these pies."

"It's a good thing you didn't," Theo said. "Then what would we have put the candle in when we sing to you?"

I gave him an amused glance. "Wait a minute. Are you saying this pie is my birthday 'cake?' You made me bring my own birthday cake to my party?"

Theo threw back his head and laughed. "Why not? Your pie is better than any cake I could have bought, and you know it. Besides, I needed an excuse to get you out here."

I shook my head at him. "You really are a rascal."

Mitch, who must have been feeling nervous over the fact that Theo was standing so close to me, chose that moment to jump into the conversation. "Alright, let's get this party started. It's time to celebrate Izzy!"

Theo nodded in agreement, and disappeared into the back of the tasting room. He came back out trailed by several of his employees, who held large platters of food. Within minutes, a huge buffet was set up in the room, and festive music was streaming from the room's speakers. I was hugged and given well-wishes by everyone as they made their way to load up plates of food. Finally, Mitch, the last of the well-wishers, approached me.

"Happy early birthday," he said, raising a glass of wine in my direction. "I hope your next year is filled with a bit calmer adventures than this year was."

I laughed. "We'll see what happens. But thank you. It is nice to have a moment of calm. Did you get a confession from George?"

He nodded. "He caved and gave us a full confession in hopes of getting a lighter sentence. But he'll still be going away to jail for a long, long time. I know Tiffany is glad about that. She feels vindicated, and she's happy that Big Al is getting justice. Of course,

Apple Crumble Assault

nothing will bring him back, but it does help her to know that George didn't get away with this."

"She does look a lot happier today," I said as I glanced in her direction. "But what about Jenny? Was Jenny happy to hear of George's arrest as well?"

Mitch shrugged. "I suppose. But she has her own problems to deal with now. We found out that what Tiffany was saying was true: Jenny was running a drug operation, so she's in some legal trouble of her own now. She'll be going off to prison for quite some time, too—although not for nearly as long as George."

"Truffle?" a chipper voice interrupted just then. Mitch and I both looked in the direction the voice had come from and saw that Bruce was standing there with a tray of truffles.

"Bruce!" I exclaimed, suddenly feeling awkward. "It's good to see you. I hope there aren't any hard feelings between us since I exposed your secret hideout. Hopefully you can understand that I was just trying to follow all leads on the case."

I bit my lower lip, worried that Bruce was going to tell me off. But instead, he smiled and handed me a truffle. "Nonsense. I owe you a big debt of gratitude. It turns out that folks don't actually care that my truffles don't come from France. In fact, a lot of people think it's cool to have 'locally grown' truffles. My restaurant is more popular than ever, and I have you to thank for it. I never would have had the guts to go public with my secret if I hadn't been forced to let the police investigate my hideout."

I smiled and popped the truffle into my mouth. "I'm glad it all worked out, then. I hope your restaurant continues to see success."

Bruce winked at me. "And I hope you and your man continue to see success in your relationship."

I looked over at Mitch, who looked surprised, and then we both laughed.

"No, it's not like that," I said. "Mitch and I aren't dating."

"Not that I wouldn't be willing to," Mitch hurriedly added.

Bruce looked amused. "No, I don't mean Mitch, of course. I mean Theo."

Bruce pointed behind me, and I turned around to see Theo approaching us with a smile on his face. I turned back toward Bruce.

"Oh, no! It's not like that, either," I said. But Bruce was already gone, and Theo laughed.

"I see Bruce still thinks we're a thing," Theo said with a laugh.

"It's not funny!" I said. "He's going to keep telling people about us and before you know it everyone in town will think we're dating."

"And would that be such a bad thing?" Theo asked, wiggling an eyebrow at me.

"Yes!" Mitch and I both exclaimed in unison.

Theo only laughed again. "You'll have to choose one of us eventually."

I crossed my arms and shook my head at him. "No I won't. I'm perfectly capable of taking care of myself."

"But then who will you dance with at parties like this?" Theo said, holding out his hand. "Come on. Come dance with me. You know you want to."

But just then, a feisty hand with hot pink fingernails slapped Theo's hand away. I looked up and saw Grams grinning at me. "She can always dance with me."

Grams pulled me away from the two men and toward a makeshift dance floor that had been set up on one side of the tasting room. She started boogying better than most of the people on that dance floor who were half her age. I laughed, and started boogying right along with her.

"I thought you wanted me to choose Theo," I said as we danced.

Grams winked at me. "I want you to choose whoever you want. I think Theo is a good catch, but if you're not ready, then you're not ready. Now let's have some fun!"

"Don't forget about me!" Molly said, dancing up to us. "I want to have fun, too!"

"Where's Scott?" I asked.

She grinned. "Still at the buffet. But I'm ready to dance."

"Me too," Tiffany said, somewhat shyly as she approached our group. I smiled welcomingly at her, and soon the four of us were dancing our hearts out together.

It was the best birthday party I'd ever had, and it was made all the better by the fact that Big Al's murder case was solved thanks to my sleuthing efforts.

Part of me wanted to tell Molly, Grams, and Tiffany that I was hanging up my detective hat for good after all the excitement of this case. But part of me knew that I wouldn't be able to resist if another mystery came along.

And although things were quiet in Sunshine Springs at the moment, they never stayed that way for long—but I wouldn't have it any other way.

ABOUT THE AUTHOR

Diana DuMont lives and writes in Northern California. When she's not reading or dreaming up her latest mystery plot, she can usually be found hiking in the nearby redwood forests. You can connect with her at www.dianadumont.com.

Made in the USA
Columbia, SC
29 September 2020